EVA

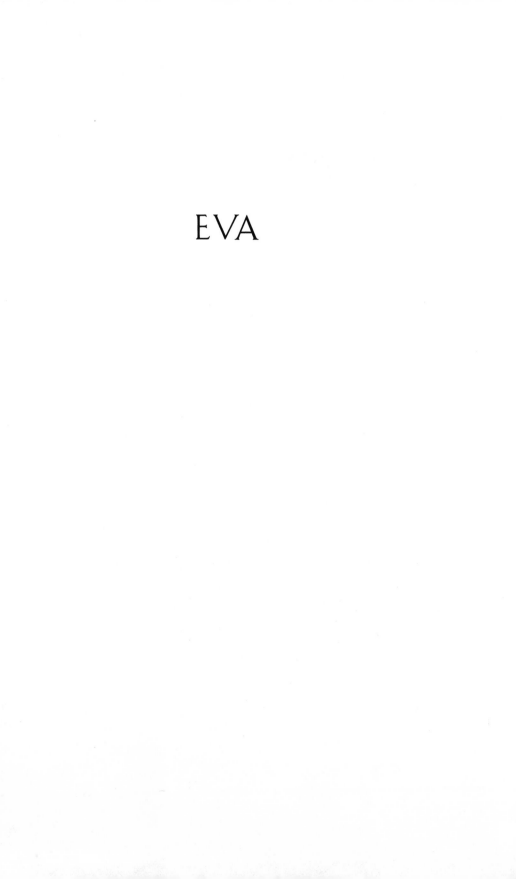

By the same author:

FOR YOUNG PEOPLE
The Changes Trilogy:
THE WEATHERMONGER
HEARTSEASE
THE DEVIL'S CHILDREN

·

EMMA TUPPER'S DIARY
THE DANCING BEAR
THE GIFT
CHANCE, LUCK AND DESTINY
THE BLUE HAWK
ANNERTON PIT
HEPZIBAH
TULKU
CITY OF GOLD AND OTHER
STORIES FROM THE OLD TESTAMENT
THE SEVENTH RAVEN
HEALER
GIANT COLD
A BOX OF NOTHING
MERLIN DREAMS

FOR ADULTS

THE GLASS-SIDED ANTS' NEST
THE OLD ENGLISH PEEP SHOW
THE SINFUL STONES
SLEEP AND HIS BROTHER
THE LIZARD IN THE CUP
THE GREEN GENE
THE POISON ORACLE
THE LIVELY DEAD
KING AND JOKER
WALKING DEAD
ONE FOOT IN THE GRAVE
THE LAST HOUSEPARTY
HINDSIGHT
DEATH OF A UNICORN
TEFUGA
PERFECT GALLOWS

EVA

PETER DICKINSON

Delacorte
Press

To Jane Goodall

Published by
Delacorte Press
Bantam Doubleday Dell Publishing Group, Inc.
666 Fifth Avenue
New York, New York 10103

This work was originally published in Great Britain
by Victor Gollancz Ltd.

Library of Congress Cataloging in Publication Data

Dickinson, Peter
Eva / Peter Dickinson.
p. cm.
ISBN 0-385-29702-5
[1. Chimpanzees—Fiction.   2. Transplantation of organs, tissues,
etc.—Fiction.   3. Animals—Treatment—Fiction.]   I. Title.
PZ7.D562Ev   1989   88-29435
[Fic]—dc19   CIP
                                                                        AC

Manufactured in the United States of America

April 1989

10 9 8 7 6 5 4 3 2 1

BG

EVA

PART ONE
WAKING

DAY ONE

Waking . . .
Strange . . .
Dream about trees? Oh, come back! Come . . .
Lost . . .
But so strange . . .

Eva was lying on her back. That was strange enough. She always slept facedown. Now she only knew that she wasn't by the sensation of upness and downness—she couldn't actually feel the pressure of the mattress against her back. She couldn't feel anything. She couldn't be floating? Still dreaming?

When she tried to feel with a hand if the mattress was there, it wouldn't move. Nothing moved! Stuck!

In panic she forced her eyes open. It seemed a huge effort. Slowly the lids rose.

Dim white blur. A misty hovering shape, pale at the center, dark at the edges.

"Darling?"

With a flood of relief Eva dragged herself out of the nightmare. Mom's voice. The mist unblurred a little, and the shape was Mom's face. She could see the blue eyes and the mouth now.

She tried to smile, but her lips wouldn't move.

"It's all right, darling. You're going to be all right."

There was something terrible in the voice.

"Do you know me, darling? Can you understand what I'm saying? Close your eyes and open them again."

The lids moved slow as syrup. When she opened them she could see better, Mom's face almost clear, but still just blur beyond.

"Oh, darling!"

Relief and joy in the voice now but something else still, underneath.

"You're going to be all right, darling. Don't worry. You've been unconscious for . . . for a long time. Now you're going to start getting better. You aren't really paralyzed. You can't move anything except your eyes yet, but you will soon, little by little, until you're running about again, good as new."

Eva closed her eyes. A picnic? Yes, on the seashore—Dad standing at the wave edge, holding Grunt's hand on one side and Bobo's on the other, all three shapes almost black against the glitter off the ripples. And after that? Nothing.

"Is she asleep?" whispered Mom.

As Eva opened her eyes she heard a faint electronic mutter, and this time she could see clearly enough to notice a thing like a hearing aid tucked in under the black coil of hair by Mom's left ear.

"I don't know if you can remember the accident, darling. We're all right too, Dad and me, just a bit bruised. Grunt broke his wrist—the chimps got loose in the car, you see—on the way back from the seashore. Can you remember? One blink for yes and two for no, all right?"

Eva opened and closed the heavy lids, twice.

"Oh, darling, it's so wonderful to have you back! I've only got five minutes, because I mustn't wear you out, and then they'll put you back to sleep for a while. Look, this is a toy they've made for you, until you're really better."

She held up a small black keyboard.

"They're going to start letting you move your left hand in a day or two," she said. "If everything goes well, I mean. So you can use this to do things for yourself, like switching the shaper off and on. What's the code for that?"

She'd asked the question to the air. The mutter answered. She pressed a few keys, and a zone hummed out of sight at the foot of the bed. At the same time a mirror in the ceiling directly above Eva's head began to move, showing her first a patch of carpet and then the corner of some kind of machine that stood close by the foot of the bed and then the zone as it sprang to life. It must have been a news program or something, an immense crowd stretching away along a wide street, banners, the drifting trails of tear gas, cries of rage . . .

"We don't want *that*," said Mom and switched off, then listened as the little speaker muttered at her ear.

"All right," she said. "Darling, they say it's time for me to go. It's been so wonderful . . . I never believed . . . I'll just open the blind for you, okay?, so that you've got something to look at next time you wake up . . ."

Eva had closed her eyes to answer yes, but the lids didn't seem to want to open. She heard the slats of the blind rattle up and a slight whine directly overhead as the mirror tilted to show her the window.

"Oh, darling," said Mom's voice, farther away now. There was something in it—had been all along, in spite of the happiness in the words. A difficulty, a sense of effort . . .

A door opened and closed. For a while Eva lay with her eyes shut, expecting to drift off to sleep, back into the dream, but stopped by the need to try and puzzle out what Mom had told her. There'd been an accident in the car on the way back from the picnic, caused by the chimps getting loose. Grunt probably—he was always up to something. She'd been unconscious since then, and now she was lying here, in some kind of hospital probably, unable to move. But it was going to be all right. They were going to let her start moving her left hand in a day or two, and then later on the rest of her, little by little . . .

Really? Mom wouldn't have lied—she never did. If it had been Dad, now . . .

Her forehead tried to frown but wouldn't move. She'd heard of people being paralyzed after accidents, and then parts of them getting better, but the doctors *letting* it happen . . . ?

And the keyboard and the mirror—that showed it was going to take a long time, or they wouldn't have bothered . . .

Something was dragging her down toward darkness. She willed herself awake. She fought to open her eyes. They wouldn't. But almost . . .

A reason to open them . . . something to see . . . the window, Mom had said. She must look out of the window, see . . .

Suckingly the lids heaved up. A blur of bright light, clearing, clearing, and now a white ceiling with a large mirror tilted to show the window. The light dazzled. After the long darkness it was almost like pain, but Eva forced herself to stare through it, waiting for her eyes to adapt to the glare. Now there was mist still, but it was in the mirror. An enormous sky, pale, pale blue. Light streaming sideways beneath it, glittering into diamonds where it struck the windows of the nearer buildings. High rise beyond high rise, far into the distance, all rising out of mist, the familiar, slightly brownish floating dawn mist that you always seemed to get in the city at the start of a fine day. She must be a long way up in a high rise herself, she could see so far. Later on, as the city's half-billion inhabitants began to stir about the streets the mist would rise, thinning as it rose, becoming just a haze but stopping you from seeing more than the first few dozen buildings. But now under the clear dawn sky in the sideways light of a winter sunrise Eva could see over a hundred kilometers, halfway perhaps to the farther shore where the city ended. She felt a sudden surge of happiness, of contentment to have awakened on such a perfect morning. It was like being born again. A morning like the first morning in the world.

In the room beyond, a door had opened and closed, and Eva's mother had come through. Her face was lined and her shoulders sagged with effort. There were four other people in the room. A man with a blond beard, graying slightly, sat watching a shaper zone that showed the scene Eva's mother had just left, the small figure on the white hospital bed ringed by its attendant machines and lit by the sunrise beyond the window. A younger man and woman in lab coats sat at computer consoles with a battery of VDUs in front of them, and an older woman in a thick, stained sweater and lopsided skirt stood at their shoulders, watching the displays.

Eva's mother settled herself onto the arm of the first man's chair and put her hand into his.

"Well done," he whispered.

There was silence for a minute.

"She doesn't want to go to sleep," said the man at the console. "Trying to get her eyes open."

"Let her," said the older woman.

The shape in the zone raised its eyelids. Clear brown eyes stared up. Slowly the wide pupils contracted.

"She knew me," said Eva's mother. "At least she knew me."

The older woman turned at her voice and came over to stand beside her, looking down at the zone.

"Yes, she certainly knew you, Mrs. Adamson," she said. "You were the first thing she saw and recognized. That was essential. Now she is seeing a familiar view. That can do nothing but good."

"If only she could smile or something. If only I could feel she was happy."

"I cannot let her use her face muscles for a long while yet.

She must not attempt to speak until most of her main bodily functions are firmly reimplanted. But for happiness . . . Ginny! A microshot of endorphin. And then put her back to sleep.''

Eva's mother started to sob. The older woman patted clumsily at her shoulder.

"Don't cry, Mrs. Adamson," she said. "It's going to be all right. We've brought it off, in spite of everything. Your daughter's all there.''

She turned and went back to the control area. The man rose and followed her. They stood watching the displays and talking in low voices. But Eva's mother sat motionless, staring at the zone, searching for a signal, the hint of a message, while beyond the imaged window the image of sunrise brightened into the image of day.

DAY SIX

Waking again . . .
Still strange . . .
Stranger each time, more certainly strange . . .
But surely the dream had been there, unchanged.
The trees . . .
Lost . . .
Loster than ever . . .

Already Eva had gotten into a waking habit. She would keep her eyes shut and try to remember something about the dream and fail. Then she would feel with her left hand for the keyboard and check that she'd left the mirror angled toward the window and that nobody had come in and changed it while she'd been asleep. And then, still with her eyes shut, she'd guess what time of day or night it was—they let her stay awake for more than an hour now, and then put her back to sleep for a while and woke her up again, so it might be any time—and what the weather was. And last of all she'd open her eyes and see if she'd guessed right.

First, what time? Not where were the hands on the clock, but where was the sun? Up *there.* It didn't seem like guessing. She could sense the presence of the sun, almost like a pressure, a weight, despite the layers of high rise above her. The weather, though? She didn't feel so sure about that, but it had been sunny the last few wakings, so a fine day, late morning . . .

She opened her eyes.

Dead right. The sun up *there.* She could tell by the stretching shadows under the sills of the high rise of the university library. The city haze was more than halfway up the nearer high rises, and as it thickened with distance it seemed to become deeper, so that only the tops of the farther buildings showed here and there, like rocks in a sea, and beyond that they vanished altogether. Nice guess, Eva—only it wasn't a guess. Funny how sure she felt about the sun. She couldn't remember that happening before the accident.

Next, she practiced using the keyboard. Mom had called it a toy, but if so it was an extremely expensive one. A very clever gadget indeed. It lay strapped in place beneath her hand, and the keys were so arranged that she could reach all of them. It didn't just do the things Mom had said, like moving the mirror and switching the shaper off and on and changing channels—its chief trick was that she could use it to talk. Only very slowly, so far. First you pressed a couple of keys to set it to the "Talk" mode, and then you tapped out what you wanted to say in ordinary English spelling, and then you coded for "Tone," and last of all you pressed the "Speak" bar, and it spoke.

It spoke not with a dry electronic rasp but with a human voice, Eva's real voice, taken from old home-shaper discs and sorted into all its possible sounds and stored in a memory to be used any way she wanted. It was tricky, like learning to play the violin or something. Practice wasn't just getting her hand to know the keys and then work faster and faster; it was also putting in a sentence and then getting the voice to say it in different ways ("Mary *had* a little lamb!" "*Mary* had a little lamb?" "Mary had a leetle lamb.").

Dad said it had been especially built for her by scientists in the Communications Faculty. His blue eyes, paler and harder than Mom's, had sparkled with excitement while he showed her its tricks—it was just his sort of toy. Eva, to be honest, had

been less excited—okay, the scientists were friends of Dad's—
the Chimp Pool was technically part of the university, and
this room was in the Medical Faculty—and they'd been
amused to see what they could do. Even so it must mean,
surely, that nobody expected her to start speaking properly for
a long time—months. Years? Ever? But Mom had said . . .

No she hadn't. She'd talked about running around, not
about speaking.

The thought came and went as Eva practiced, until suddenly she got irritated with her slowness and switched the
shaper on instead. A thriller of some sort—a woman desperately pushing her way in the wrong direction along a crowded
traveler—not that. A flivver-rally, the sky patterned with
bright machines, the buzz of thousands of rotors—not that. A
beach, kilometers of shoreline invisible under human bodies,
the white surf bobbing with human heads—not that. People,
people, people. Ah, trees . . .

Only a cartoon, actually, one she used to watch a lot when
she was smaller, because of the heroine's name. It was called
Adam and Eve and the plot was always the same. Adam and
Eve were the first people, and they were king and queen of the
jungle. Adam ruled the animals, and Eve ruled the plants.
Their enemy was the Great Snake. Adam and Eve were trying
to drive him out of their jungle, so that it would be safe for
them to have children, but Adam was always getting into
trouble—usually a trap set by the Great Snake—because of his
arrogance and impulsiveness, and then Eve had to get him out
of it by her plant magic. It was rather wishy-washy but pretty
to look at. All around the world hundreds of millions of little
girls waited in ecstasy for the moment when Eve would begin
her plant magic. Dad said the company spent huge amounts
on research to make sure they put in what little girls wanted.

Now Eva watched, pleased by the greenness and the shapes
of leaf and branch. Eve was following a trail through the

jungle. Adam was in a mess somewhere, no doubt. The plants moved twigs and tendrils to show Eve the way he'd gone. She came to a cave mouth. She put a seed in the earth and caused a flower to spring up, a single white cup like a shaper dish. A huge white moth came out of the cave to drink at the nectar from the flower, and then guided Eve down into the darkness, using the trail of pollen that had stuck to Adam's feet as he came swishing through the jungle . . .

Eva lost patience and switched off. It was funny, she thought, these sudden surges of annoyance—twice now this morning. She never used to be like that. She didn't feel like practicing with her voice again, so for something to do she told the mirror to go back and show her the view. She watched the reflections as it swung to its new position, mostly carpet and the corners of things, a piece of the cart, one of the machines that monitored and fed her and took her waste away, the air-conditioner, the window. The forest of high rises, the millions of people, people, people . . .

The crammed streets, the crammed beaches, the crammed skies—they were only a fraction of them. Most people stayed in their rooms all day, just to get away from one another. A lot of them never went out at all. Their world was four walls and their shaper zone. Dad said that the shaper companies were the real rulers of the world. The people told them what they wanted and the companies gave it to them and nothing else mattered. The view from the window was beautiful, until you thought about the people.

Eva lost patience again and told the mirror to go somewhere else. The only place it knew was the visitor's chair. She watched as it swung—the air-conditioner, the machine, the cart, the blank zone, another machine, the chair . . .

The long way around—it could have gone straight across the bed . . .

Why . . . ?

They didn't want her to see the bed!

That note in Mom's voice, the effort, the sorrow. The keyboard, the trouble they'd taken. The way they'd set the mirror. The accident. You can get very badly smashed in an accident.

"What a pretty baby!" strangers used to say. "What a lovely little girl!" Later, just looks and smiles that said the same—glances and stares from boys when she came into a new class. She'd had Mom's oval face but Dad's high cheekbones, eyes a darker blue than either of them, long black gleaming hair, straight nose, full mouth . . . She'd moved like a dancer, easily, fallen without thought into graceful poses . . .

No!

But she had to know, to see. Urgently she moved the mirror again, back to the window. It swung the whole way around, of course. She tried confusing it, stopping it, giving it fresh instructions before it had finished a movement. No good . . .

The door opened and shut, and Mom was standing by the bed. She was pale. Her mass of hair was a mess, with a lot of gray showing in the glossy black. There were hard lines down beside her nostrils. She looked as though she hadn't slept for a year. Her smile wasn't real.

"Hello, my darling," she whispered. "I'm sorry I'm late. How are you today?"

She bent and kissed Eva on her numb forehead. A strand of her hair trailed across Eva's face. It didn't tickle, because the face was numb too, but Eva automatically closed that eye to let it pass. Mom turned away to get the tall stool so that she could sit by the bed where Eva could see her directly. Eva's eyelids still moved rather sluggishly, so she didn't open the shut one at once.

Hey!

She opened it and closed the other one. Then the first

again. Mom had come back now and slid her hand under the bedclothes to grasp Eva's own hand.

"What are you doing, you funny girl?"

Eva answered the cool grip with a squeeze, but she could feel Mom's jumpiness, and hear the false note in the lightness she tried to put into her voice. Her hand was wrong too. Too small. Deep in the nightmare now, Eva stared up into Mom's questioning eyes. They were wrong too, something different about the color. She forced herself to close one eye again and then the other, squinting inwardly as she did so.

Her nose was gone.

Most of the time you don't see your nose at all; but if you shut one eye and look sideways, there it is, that fuzzy hummock, too close to focus. It was gone. At the lower rim of vision she could see the vague blur of a cheek and at the top the darker fringe of an eyebrow, much more noticeable— much more *there*—than it used to be . . .

Mom wasn't even pretending to smile now.

Eva closed both eyes and willed the nightmare into day. The accident. Her whole face must have been so badly smashed that they couldn't rebuild it, or not yet anyway. They were keeping it numb so that it didn't hurt. Her jaw and mouth must be so bad that she wouldn't be able to speak right for ages—never perhaps—so they'd made her her voice box instead. They didn't want her to see herself in the mirror . . .

She wriggled her fingers out of Mom's grip and slowly found the right keys. No point in fussing with tones. She pressed the "Speak" bar.

"Let me see," said her voice, dead flat.

"Darling . . ." croaked Mom.

A whisper rustled in the speaker by her ear. She stopped to listen. Eva pressed out another message.

"Let me see. Or I'll go mad. Wondering."

"She's right," said Mom to the air. "No, it's too late . . .
No."

The murmur started again. Eva gripped Mom's hand again
and closed her eyes. Why was the hand so small? Had her own
hand . . . The thumb was all wrong! Why hadn't she noticed? It was . . .

Without her touching the keys, the mirror motor whined.
She kept her eyes closed until it stopped.

"I love you, darling," said Mom. "I love you."

Eva willed her eyes to open.

For an instant all she seemed to see was nightmare. Mess. A
giant spiderweb, broken and tangled on the pillows, with the
furry black body of the spider dead in the middle of it. And
then the mess made sense.

She closed her right eye and watched the brown left eye in
the mirror close as she did so. The web—it wasn't broken—
was tubes and sensor wires connecting the machines around
the bed to the pink-and-black thing in the center. She stared.
Her mind wouldn't work. She couldn't think, only feel—feel
Mom's tension, Mom's grief, as much as her own amazement.
Poor Mom—her lovely blue-eyed daughter . . . Must do
something for Mom. She found the right keys.

"Okay," said her voice. "It's okay, Mom."

"Oh, my darling," said Mom and started to cry. That was
okay too. Mom cried easy, usually when the worst was over.
Eva stared at the face in the mirror. She'd recognized it at
once, but couldn't give it a name. Then it came. Carefully she
pressed the keys. She used the tone control to sound cheerful.

"Hi, Kelly," said her voice.

Kelly was—had been—a young female chimpanzee.

Eva had grown up with chimps.

As more and more people crammed into the world, needing
more and more land for cities and crops, so the animals had

died out. Most of the great wild jungles were gone, and the savannahs that used to cover half a continent. Here and there a few patches of jungle remained, among mountains too steep to use, or stretches of bleak and barren upland unsuitable for the energy fields that filled most of the old hot deserts, or offshore waters where fish farms for some reason wouldn't flourish, but even these were always being nibbled away as somebody found a new method of exploiting them. And anyway, the wild animals that had been crowded into those pockets had destroyed them by their numbers or become diseased or just seemed to lose interest in living in a world like that.

The big animals vanished first, elephants and giraffes, gorillas and orangs, whales and dolphins. Others hung on in the patches and crannies people left for them by mistake or on purpose. A few actually throve because living in a world full of people suited them in ways they could adapt to—there were no eagles anymore, but you could see kestrels any day in the city, nesting among the high rises or hovering in the updrafts between them, living off mice and sparrows and other small creatures, which in turn lived off the scraps that people littered around. There were rats, of course, and wasps and city pigeons and starlings and so on, but that was all.

There'd been zoos for a while, but what was the point of going to see a few sad old elephants in an enclosure when you could go to a shaper park and walk among the shapes of an elephant herd, life-sized, wallowing in the shape of a mud pool while the shape of a lion stalked the shape of an eland beyond (all stored on old tapes, made before the last savannahs had gone)? And at home there were wild-life programs on the shaper, either old tapes or live from the little patches of jungle and desert that still were left. You could have them in your living room, hear their screams and songs, watch their hunting and mating. They weren't life-sized, of course, and you couldn't smell them, and when they killed and ate one another, the blood disappeared from your carpet as soon as you switched channels. Besides, a real rhinoceros, living the life it was made for, needs a dozen square kilometers. A taped rhinoceros only needs a few cubic centimeters. So it was all very tidy and sensible, just right for a world crammed full of people. That's what people had thought, until it was too late. And that is why there were only the chimps left.

Chimps were different. Chimps were a special case because they were so close to humans, our cousins but not us. It was worth keeping real chimps alive for research you couldn't do on humans, a pool of chimps big enough to breed from, so that there were animals to spare for scientists to use. Of course, now that they'd lost all the other big animals, now that they'd found that shapings, however solid-seeming, weren't really a substitute, people had become interested in real chimps. More than interested—obsessed, almost. Easily the most popular commercials on the shaper were for a soft drink called Honeybear that used live chimps dressed up as people. All the cities had branches of the International Chimp Pool where you could go and see a few chimps in big cages. But the main sections of the Pool were right here, part of the university, and Eva's dad was Director of Primate Zoology, in charge of research. So Eva had grown up among chimps.

In fact, she'd been one of Dad's research projects. Of course, she'd met humans her own age because Mom and Dad, like other parents, put their child into playgroups so that she would learn to socialize, but Eva had always felt just as at home among chimps. In some ways more, in fact—she'd been making chimp chatter before she said her first human word, and before she was three Dad had been using her to help him understand how the chimps' minds were working. He knew almost everything there was to know about them, from the outside, but Eva could joke with their jokes, feel with their feelings, see why some simple-to-humans problem baffled them when they could solve trickier-looking problems almost at once.

Of course, Mom and Dad had needed to be careful. A small chimp is enormously stronger than a human baby; it's even smarter for the first few months; but Eva had soon learned how to behave, how to use the grunts and gestures that meant "You're the boss" and "Please" and "Sorry, didn't mean it," and so on. She'd gotten along with chimps pretty well, always.

And now she was one herself. Okay.

She felt a sort of mild amazement. All her feelings were calm, a bit dreamy. They must be pumping something into her bloodstream, she reckoned, to control her shock and rejection. This must be real panic time for them out there, whoever they were who whispered into the little speaker in Mom's ear. Anyway, there were questions to ask. She pressed keys.

"How . . . ?"

No need to say any more with Mom. With Dad you'd have had to spell the question right out, but Mom was used to hints and garblings because she worked in the Housing Bureau, helping ordinary people straighten out ordinary problems like back rent or rowdy neighbors or trying to get away with an unlicensed pregnancy.

"It's something called neuron memory, darling," said Mom. "Dad says you'll have learned about it at school, so you probably know more than me. You were in an irreversible coma after the accident, and Joan Pradesh heard about it and said she'd try and . . . and do *this*, if we wanted. She's never done a human before, you see. It was a risk, she said, but we thought, in the end . . . well . . . your poor body, it was so broken, and just lying there . . . anyway, we said yes. And it's worked. That's marvelous, isn't it? But now you've got to be very patient and just lie and wait for all the connections to strengthen, one after another. You're there. You're joined up.

But the connections aren't strong enough to use yet. Have I got that right?''

She'd asked the question to the air. The speaker began its whisper.

Neuron memory, thought Eva. Joan Pradesh. Of course. And yes, she had studied it at school last year. The thing is, you aren't just a lot of complicated molecules bundled together inside a skin—you're that too, but that's not what makes you *you*. What *you* are is a pattern, an arrangement, different from any other pattern that ever was or will be. Your pattern began to grow from the moment you were conceived, but the things that make you so sure you are *you* came later: your discoveries of the world, from your first blurred peerings with your baby eyes, and all your thoughts and imaginings and dreams and memories make up that pattern, and are kept there by the neurons in your brain that have sent their wriggling axons and dendrites branching and joining and passing messages to one another through the incredible complex networks they have grown into. What old Professor Pradesh, Joan's father, had found was that the pattern actually "remembers" how it got there; and given the right treatment and an "empty" brain, it can be persuaded to go through the whole process over again. Professor Pradesh had made his discovery with very simple creatures, flatworms mainly, but Joan had carried on the research until she was working with mammals, all the way up to chimps. And now, humans.

Eva pressed a few keys.

"How long?" said her voice.

"Two hundred and thirty-eight days."

It was the wrong answer, for once. Even so, Eva's mind juddered with the thought. Eight whole months gone from your life, blank! Of course, it would take that long for the pattern to grow—in the first Eva it had taken almost fourteen years.

"No," she said. "How long till?"

"Sorry," said Mom. "It was just . . ."

Of course. Mom knew the exact count of days. She'd felt each of them grind through her, never knowing if the risk would be worth it or if she'd get no more than part of her daughter back or perhaps just a mumbling kind of nobody trapped in Kelly's body. No wonder she looked so much older. The speaker whisper stopped. Mom nodded.

"Joan's been saying you mustn't try and start waking muscles up before they're ready. You must try not even to think about it. Just let it happen. She wasn't really ready for you to find out what . . . what's happened, but now you *have* found out she's probably going to change her plans and start letting you move your face muscles. She didn't want to before because you'd have tried to talk . . ."

The whisper started again. Eva lay looking at the face in the mirror. Me, she thought. Not Kelly, me. Good-bye, blue eyes, good-bye soft pale skin, good-bye, nose. Perhaps Kelly had been pretty—pretty to another chimp. Except that chimps didn't seem to think like that, judging by the way the males used to go mad about moth-eaten old Rosie when she was in season . . .

The brown eyes peered down in the way you might gaze at an animal. Was there a glimmer there? Eva, inside?

Mom sighed and squared her shoulders, ready to explain yet more, but Eva closed her eyes. She was tired, tired of newness and strangeness and the world of people. She made her voice say "No." Not enough. With an effort she chose more keys. All she wanted to do was hide, vanish, creep away into dark green shadows.

"Sleep now, please," said her voice.

They let her go gently. Her last thought was to wonder what had happened to Kelly, the real Kelly, the one who used to live in this furry skin. Where was *she* now?

DAY SEVEN

Waking again . . .
The dream . . .
Keep it. Hold on. Hold on . . .
Waking.

Perhaps they'd let her wake gently, so that the dream had
floated up with her almost at the surface, or perhaps it was
just the idea of holding, because that was one of the things in
the dream, but at any rate Eva awoke and found that this time
she could really remember what she'd been dreaming. It was
still very strange, not like any of the dreams she usually had.
There was no story, no adventures, only the idea, the images,
the feelings—herself, moving among branches, reaching with
long arms, swinging, holding . . .

Holding with her feet if she chose.

She lay with her eyes shut, living the dream again. Then,
instead of angling the mirror to show her the window, left it
where it had been when they sent her to sleep. She opened
her eyes and looked.

The blind was up and morning light streamed across the
bed. The face in the mirror, surrounded by its tangle of tubes
and cables, was still that of a stranger. Large pale ears stuck
out on either side through strong black hair; in the middle
was the pinky-brown hummock of the face parts, with the
huge lips, the nothing nose and the forward-facing nostrils;
the brown eyes were bright with thought. She pressed keys.
Deliberately she filled her mind with ideas of welcome.

"Hi, there," said her voice.

Was there a glimmer in the eyes? Kelly's answer? Or just the reflection of Eva's own signal? No knowing.

"You've never seen a tree," she said.

That might not be quite true. The chimps in the Research Section of the Pool had metal-and-plastic frames to climb on, but Dad always took a couple on family outings if he could, so Kelly might have seen trees in the city parks, but she'd certainly not have been allowed to climb one because of the difficulty of getting her down and the damage she might do while she was up there. In any case, those would have been city trees, tamed, guarded, numbered, precious. The trees in the dream had been wild, part of a forest no one looked after, tree tangled into tree, stretching on and on, a forest where people had never been, a forest before there were people.

She swung the mirror to take her usual look at the city. It was a duller day, with the last lights just going out as the sun rose behind high thin cloud and the city's own haze, the dust and fumes made by half a billion people living and working together, beginning to form among the high rises. She could still see about five kilometers. Nothing. The city stretched on far beyond that, far beyond sight on the clearest morning, endless. Like the forest in the dream.

Of course, Eva thought, I might have put the dream there. Me. Eva. Knowing when I went to sleep that I was living in a chimp's body, I might have put chimp arms and feet into the dream. I might have invented the forest, from things I've seen on shaper programs. Only . . .

Only I was having the dream before I knew about Kelly. And it was the same dream. Perhaps knowing just helped me think about it, hold on to it, but it was there before any of that. Perhaps it isn't my dream at all—not Eva's, I mean. Perhaps it's Kelly's.

Hi, Kelly. You there?

The mirror was angled to show the window, so she sent the unspoken message inward. She wasn't really serious. It was more of a private joke, a whimsy. Her lips twitched. She actually felt them move.

Oh, great, she thought. They're letting me have my mouth back. She moved the mirror to show her the bed again and tried a smile. The image above her wrinkled its mouth at the corners.

There was a game you could play with small chimps before they became too strong for you to hold still. You put the chimp on your lap, gripping its arms to stop it from grabbing, and then you moved a grape across in front of its face and watched a sort of wave ripple along the lips from side to side, following the grape, trying to suck it in. Chimps use their long and mobile mouths almost like an extra hand for feeling and touching and trying things out, as well as for all the grimaces that make up a lot of chimp language.

Forgetting about the dream, Eva lay and experimented. There wasn't a lot she could try, because they didn't seem to have awakened her other face muscles yet, or her jaw, but it was exciting enough to be able to move anything at all. She hadn't really begun before Dad came in.

"Hi, kid," he said.

"Sorry," she tapped. "Fun."

A slight pause while he put in the missing words. You didn't get this sort of blip with Mom, but Dad thought in whole sentences, with verbs and so on.

"That's fine," he said. "Only don't push it—we'll have to see how it all goes. How are you feeling?"

"Funny. Things in my blood?"

He didn't get it.

"Stop shock?" she added.

The pause was different this time, while he decided how much to tell her.

"Well, yes," he said. "We felt it was safer. As Mom told you, your neuron linkages appear complete, but we have no way of knowing how secure they are. You have been through an extremely risky procedure, my darling. We calculated that there were about four chances in five that we would fail."

"Only hope. Or dead."

"That's right."

There was something in his tone. Dad had never been as close to Eva as Mom had, but he had loved her always and been extremely proud of her good looks. He'd kept snapshots of her in his wallet, and portrait photos in his office. Now it crossed her mind to wonder whether there'd been a funeral yet.

Dad shook his head as if he were trying to shake her picture out of his mind.

"You have to remember that with you we are in new territory," he said. "You are the first of Joan's subjects to be capable of influencing the procedure of neuron memory by conscious thought. You are the first to be properly aware of the passage of time and therefore to be able to wish to hurry the process along. You are also the first to whom we have felt the kind of moral responsibility one has toward a human being. All this means that we are going . . ."

"Hey!"

Eva had found how to make her toy do a sort of squawk that she used as a "Hey!" code. Conversations were boring if you couldn't interrupt, but it still took a second or two to work. Dad stopped, blinked, thought back.

"Of course, we have a moral responsibility to all living things," he said. "As a zoologist, life is my trade, so I feel this more strongly than most. I feel it especially toward chimpanzees. Still, it is different from the responsibility we have toward any single human being. Okay?"

Eva would have liked to argue, but it would have taken too

long and, anyway, Dad was difficult to argue with and her own thoughts were all in a mess, so she said nothing. Dad, typically, assumed she'd agreed.

"Now, the danger point does not lie in your conscious mind," he said. "You understand and can accept that what we've done was, as you said, the only hope. The danger lies at the unconscious level, over which you don't have the same control. That is why we have to control it for you, for the time being, until it too has learned to accept what has happened. It is the danger point for two reasons—first, as I say, because you can't persuade it by rational means not to reject your new body, and second, because it is itself the main interface with that body. When you think, you think with a human mind. When you blink, you blink with a chimpanzee's involuntary reaction. Your own unconscious mind lies along that border. It is not, of course, as simple as that, but that will have to do. The upshot is that we are going to have to be very cautious indeed about reducing any drugs that help suppress your unconscious tendency to rejection."

"Okay. Only little as poss."

"You will have to cooperate with Dr. Alonso, who will be your psychiatrist. Her main preoccupation in the next few weeks will be to watch out for the slightest signs that . . ."

Eva switched off. She couldn't help it. She'd been awake only about twenty minutes, but she felt exhausted already. What Dad was telling her was vital, and she should have been straining to understand every detail, but the way he did it made her mind go numb. It used to do that sometimes, even before. Dad was a natural explainer, lecturer, arranger of thoughts and facts into orderly patterns. His beard would wag, and his blue eyes—sharper and smaller than Mom's—would flash with the thrill of knowledge. His students thought he was great, which made Eva feel guilty that somehow the beard-wag and the eye-flash were like a hypnotist's signals, making her mind drift off elsewhere.

Now it drifted off to home. The three of them, Mom and Dad and Eva, having supper after some ordinary day, Dad talking, Mom listening, and Eva looking out the window and watching a million lights come on as dusk thickened across the city. Suppers must have been sad this last year, she thought. Not all families loved one another. Eva had friends one of whose parents had left, or perhaps both had stayed, but they'd bitched and quarreled. She'd been luckier than some. She'd felt pretty secure, always. But suppose something—she couldn't think what—had happened that had forced her parents to choose between their jobs and their family, well, there wouldn't have been any question with Mom; Mom was interested in her work and thought it was worth doing, but she wouldn't have hesitated. With Dad, you couldn't be sure. If he'd had to give up his work he'd have given up half himself. More than half, perhaps. So perhaps he wouldn't . . .

She looked at him as he leaned over the bed, explaining. Just beyond his head the mirror showed a bald patch in the middle of his scalp. It fascinated her. She longed to be able to sit up and rootle among the browny-gray hairs. From beyond the reflected scalp her own face gazed down. Seeing the man's head and the chimp's so close together, she was struck by a thought.

"Hey!"

Dad stopped and waited, a bit impatient.

"Kelly's brain?" said Eva. "Big enough?"

"Yes. You have, in fact, got less than you used to have, but luckily there is a bit of waste space in brains. I think you'll find you're all there, darling. Where was I? Oh, yes . . ."

But Eva had stopped listening again. The thought of grapes had returned, not out of her conscious mind but up from below. A whole bunch of grapes, purple, the bloom untouched, the skins bulging with sweet juices. Saliva spurted inside her mouth, and a machine sucked it away. She could actually feel it happening, which meant they were letting her have more of her mouth back. How long since she'd really eaten, how long since she'd had a taste on her tongue? Not since that picnic at the sea.

Dad had cocked his head to listen to the metallic whisper in his ear.

"Right," he said. "Apparently you're due for a nap, darling. Take it easy. Don't try to hurry things up, and you'll do fine. See you tomorrow, eh?"

Already Eva could feel the drift to darkness. She pressed a few keys.

"Love to Mom."

"Yes, of course."

Her eyes had closed before he was out the door. The first thing I'll ask for is grapes, she thought. Kelly would have loved grapes. All chimps do.

DAY SEVENTEEN

Waking . . .
Leaving the trees, the green shadows, the leaf light . . .
Leaving the dream . . .

But the dream itself was changing. It was Eva's fault. Sometimes even in the middle of the dream she was aware of herself as a human mind, an alien in the forest. She had thought about the dream, knowing everything the human Eva knew, so now as she reached and clambered and rested she carried the human knowledge with her.

The simplest change was that sometimes the dreams had stories. These might be a plus. She had adventures. She might look down between the branches and see men wearing clothes and carrying guns, walking on the forest floor, and she'd know the way you do in dreams that they had time-traveled from the future and were coming to cut down the forest so that a city could be built that would house the overflow of people from the bursting future world, and only Eva could stop them. Sometimes the stories were a minus. In the worst of these she was digging into a termite nest and found just below the surface a human face, Eva's own old face, gazing with blank blue eyes at the sky, still alive, but with ants going in and out of the nostrils. Mostly the dreams were neither plus nor minus but muddled, the way human dreams are. The one she called Kelly's dream hadn't been like that. It had been simple, until Eva had brought her knowledge into it. She would never have it like that again.

She dreamed ordinary human dreams too, doing and seeing things in her old body, but nearly always the one she awoke with was the one about trees. Then she would lie with her eyes shut and decide where she wanted the mirror, what would be the first thing she saw. Though she always chose the same it was still a conscious decision, an effort of will not to go back to the old game of guessing the weather. She opened her eyes and gazed up and made her voice say "Hi." As soon as they gave her her jaw and throat back, she added the proper little pant and grimace of greeting and tried to mean it. That helped.

Dad had been right. Suppose she'd awakened and seen what they'd done to her and her bloodstream hadn't been stuffed with dope to help her stand the shock, then all of her, everything that used to be Eva, would have shrieked its *No!* It would have been like that however much she'd agreed, with her conscious mind, that she wanted to live in a chimp body, that it was far better than dying. Now, as they slowly cut the dope down, she could feel that the shriek was faintly there. The morning after she'd had the ant dream—she told Dr. Alonso about that because it had scared her so much—they put the dope right back up and started again, but Eva knew she couldn't live like that forever. Kelly's body wasn't just something she had to get used to; it was something she had to learn to be happy about. Okay, it *was* better than dying, but that wasn't enough. You had to awaken and open your eyes and see your new face and like what you saw. You had to make the human greeting and the chimp greeting and mean them.

The old Eva could never have done it, the one who used to skate and ski and play volleyball at school. They'd been right to make her come to life slowly, little by little, rejoicing in having a mouth to chew with, a throat that would swallow, a real moving arm she could lift and look at. Every day, as a sort of exercise, she forced herself to think of the third Eva, the one who'd come in between, after the accident but before the waking, a sort of nothing person, a sleeping mind in a smashed body. It was *that* that she had to compare this new Eva with, not the girl who used to skate and ski. This must be better than that.

Sometimes when they removed a tube or a wire, the place where it had joined felt sore, and even that was a plus. To be hurt, you have to be alive.

Alive but clumsy. The first movements, lip-ripples and hoots and chewings, had been misleading. The morning they let her have her arm back, she awoke and realized that in her last minutes of sleep she had been caressing her hand along her hairy thigh, troubled in her dream because the fingers could feel and the thigh couldn't, so it was like stroking a rug. Then she was awake and found her whole arm moving. She had made her greetings to the face in the mirror before she realized what had happened. Gingerly she pulled the arm out and held it up with the palm half open, and saw the arm and hand in the mirror stretch down toward her in the gesture chimps make when they are asking for help or comfort. She stared at the glossy blue-black hairs, then drew the arm down and lip-nibbled comfortingly along it, thinking, So this is me now. Me. Not Kelly up in the mirror. Me down here. Okay.

When breakfast came she tried to feed herself, putting the food into her mouth. She managed it by shutting her eyes and feeling for the next morsel. From then on, the hand knew the way to the mouth. But when she tried to guide the hand by looking in the mirror, she kept going the wrong way and missing, sometimes by several centimeters. This didn't bother her much. Being able to move the arm at all was thrilling. But later that morning she found it wasn't just the confusion of trying to do things in a mirror that had been spoiling her aim.

They must have decided to give her a nap—they could still

do that. Then they woke her up, and she opened her eyes to see a stranger smiling down at her, a gorgeous young man with gleaming even teeth and a thin mustache and brown skin like polished leather.

"Hi, Eva," he said. "I'm Robbo. I'm from Space-tech."

"Uh?"

(When she'd first gotten her voice back Eva had experimented, trying to say a few human words, but it had been such an effort and her voice had come out so slow and stupid that she'd settled for chimp grunts. You could say quite a bit with those.)

"Okay, okay," said Robbo. "We're not shipping you off to colonize Vega Three. That's what I was trained for, teaching ordinary folks like you and me—"

He said it without a flicker. He was clever as well as pretty.

"—how to use their bodies when they're upside. Trouble is, there's not so much of that happening just now, so my firm has lent me across to try and give you a hand. Right?"

He bent out of sight; but watching in the mirror, Eva saw him joining some steel rods into a structure that turned out, when he rose and stood it by the bed, to be a framework suspending a cord above her chest. He clipped a blue ball to the end of the cord.

"Let's see you touch that without moving it," he said.

Eva lifted her arm and stretched it out. Her fingers bumped into the ball a good five centimeters before she expected. She clicked irritation.

"Oh, not that bad," said Robbo. "Give it another try."

He steadied the ball and she tried again. And again and again. By concentrating hard she learned to touch the ball without moving it, but this was only by learning exactly how far to stretch, not by judging the distance and getting it right. As soon as he told her to speed up, she started overreaching again. She stopped and felt for her keyboard.

"Got two arms," she said.

"Sure, like everyone else. Only your other one's supposed to be still asleep."

"No. Two this side."

"Right. They told me you might, only I didn't want to put the idea into your mind. One's a sort of ghost, uh?"

Eva grunted. That was exactly the word. Ghost. The ghost of a human arm still trying to work, to reach and touch at the mind's command. You couldn't see it but it was there, moving slightly out of synch as the chimp arm moved, with the elbow wrong and the invisible fingertips wavering among the chimp knuckles. When she closed her eyes she saw in her mind the pale slim fingers, helpless, trapped in this strange hairy place, lost. Mustn't think like that. Mustn't.

"Want to give it a rest?" said Robbo.

She grunted a No, and this time as soon as he'd steadied the ball she snaked her arm out, fast as she could move it, not giving her mind time to think about the task. She missed, but by less than a centimeter.

"Not bad," said Robbo.

After a few more tries he gave her a moving target by swinging the ball around, at first in a clean pendulum curve, then in a circle, and finally making it jiggle as it swung.

"That's enough," said Robbo. "Tired, I guess."

"Uh."

"Don't worry. You've got to take things easy. We'll work some exercises out with the physios, but you're doing pretty well. Provided you move fast, uh? Mustn't give the ghost a chance."

Mustn't, thought Eva.

"You came along just the right time for me, you know. Few more weeks, and I'd have been out of a job."

"Uh?"

"That's right. Ten years ago, when I went into this, I reckoned I was set up for life. Don't mean I thought we'd be actually colonizing planets before I died, but the push would be there, the pressure to get off earth, and at least that'd mean research for us in the business. But now look, they're all giving up. The pressure's still there, but the governments are pulling out and the sponsors are pulling out and whole departments are closing down. At Space-tech alone, we've lost forty percent of our jobs in the last three years."

Eva clicked commiseration. Robbo went on talking, as much to give her a rest as anything.

"I don't know. It just doesn't make sense. There's no reason to it. It's like we've just given up. We're tired of trying. I worry about my kid, what life's going to be like for him . . ."

He got out his wallet and showed Eva a photograph of a little boy, pretty as himself, with the same glossy brown skin and dark eyes. He went on talking. Eva half listened. People, she thought—they're funny. Her fingers moved caressingly over the furriness of her chest, and somehow the thought in her mind changed from the oddness of people worrying about why they'd stopped trying to colonize planets to the oddness of people not having any real hair on their bodies, being so smooth and shiny. When she thought of him like that Robbo didn't seem pretty at all.

"Try something else?" he said at last. She grunted okay and he swung her table across the bed and gave her some colored bricks to build a tower with. She made it straight and slim, and far higher than a chimp could ever have done. Not that chimps are clumsy—they pick and groom among one another's fur with nimble, sensitive fingers—but they don't think tidy. Give them a cylinder to fit into a hole, and they'll fumble it in any old way because that's good enough. It wouldn't enter their heads to square up the edges of a pile of blocks, so they'd get it out of kilter and down it would crash. But Eva could use her human mind to tell the chimp fingers what she wanted, and check by touch that they'd got it right. When Robbo asked her to speed it up she became chimp-clumsy. By that time she was tired again, so Robbo chatted a little more and left.

She lay with her eyes shut, but as soon as she began to feel drowsy she forced them open and pressed the keys on her control box.

"Don't want to sleep," said her voice.

"Just as you like, dearie," sighed Meg's soft answer from behind the headboard.

Wakefulness came flooding back, and Eva reset the mirror to show her the window, with a rainy mild day beyond the glass. Dull gray clouds were touching the tops of the dull gray high rises, and the air in the distance hung like smoke where the rain fell dense. She felt the skin of her arm tingle as the pores closed, stirring the coarse hair as they did so, and she sensed rather than felt the rest of her numb body trying to do the same. Not long now, she thought. A few more weeks, and I'll be walking. Walking's going to be tricky—I'll be the wrong distance from the ground. No I won't—I'll be the right distance, but . . . I'm going to have to get rid of that ghost.

It was important. It was more important than just for walking without falling flat on your face. The thing is, you aren't a mind *in* a body, you're a mind *and* a body, and they're both *you.* As long as the ghost of that other body haunted her, she would never become a *you,* belonging all together, a whole person. She could probably learn how to pick things up cleanly and pour out of a bottle and run around without tripping by training herself not to notice the ghost, but it would be there still. No good.

She wondered whether to talk to Dr. Alonso about this. Dr. Alonso was all right, but Eva had taken a dislike to her. She was too kind, too cooing—it wasn't real. While she sat smiling by the bed Eva kept seeing Dr. Alonso II, tucked out of sight in the corner of the room, thin-lipped, scribbling notes for a scientific article. Anyway, she didn't actually *know* anything —nobody did, because Eva was the first of her kind, and it was all new to everyone—but at least the biochemists and neurologists and everythingelsists knew a few facts about brains and bloodstreams and nervous systems and so on, but the psychiatrists were guessing all the way. Eva thought she could guess just as well as Dr. Alonso.

So now she closed her eyes again and summoned up the dream. She lay wide awake, concentrating with all her will but letting the images float into her mind, the shapes of a green tree world, branches with bark rough or smooth, blobs and patches of sunlight seeping through the leaf cover, fruits and berries yellow, green, purple, orange, and through all this a single person, a body completely itself with its own mind part of it and the body part of the mind, reaching, grasping, swinging below a branch, finding and holding with a foot, reaching on.

Kelly was dead, gone, would never come back, but something was still there. Not a particular chimp with particular memories of a large cage with a cement floor and a steel-and-plastic climbing frame and perhaps a human who took her out to greener places on a leash, but a chimp still, with older, deeper memories. You couldn't just invade a chimp body and take it over with your human mind, like a hero in a history book—you'd never get to be whole that way. Eva's human neurons might have copied themselves into Kelly's brain, but as Dad had said, that left a sort of connection, an interface, a borderland where human ended and chimp began. You couldn't live like that, with a frontier in you like a wall, keeping your selves apart. The only way to become whole was to pull the wall down, to let the other side back in, to let it invade in its turn, up into the human side, the neurons remembering their old paths, twining themselves in among the human network until both sides made a single pattern. A new pattern, not Eva, not Kelly—both but one.

That must be why she'd started dreaming the dream, even before she had first awakened. The chimp side had been trying to find its way back. So now, wide awake, she dreamed it again. Beyond her closed eyelids, beyond the sealed window, lay the rainy world crammed with humans. Soon, in a few weeks, Eva was going to be out there herself among them, trying to fit in, to belong, to cope with the fret and bustle of the human-centered city. She could never do that unless she became whole.

Inside her hairy skull she let the forest form. It was real. It was peaceful, endless, happy. There were no humans in it.

MONTH TWO,
DAY NINETEEN

Awake . . .
Not just your eyelids rising, facing the day . . .
Your whole body, all of it, moving and feeling . . .

Carefully Eva pushed herself off the pillow and sat. With her right arm she heaved the bedclothes aside, then twisted herself till her legs dangled over the edge. All wrong. She was thinking too much. This was how a human would try to get out of bed, unaided for the first time, after a long illness. The ghost was very strong. All the shapes and distances seemed strange. Mom was watching from the chair.

"Sure you don't want me to help?" she said.

Eva rippled her fingers over the keyboard, which now lay strapped to her chest. After her weeks of practice she'd gotten the pauses down to only a couple of seconds.

"I'm fine," she said. "Been doing my exercises."

A chimp wouldn't have gotten up like this. It would have sort of rolled, and then dropped. She dropped. The ghost had judged the distance wrong, but her real limbs got it right and she didn't stagger. She climbed onto Mom's lap, giving her time to adjust the half-dozen sensor wires she still had to trail around before she kissed her. Mom laughed.

"It's like being eaten alive," she said.

Eva made her No-it's-not grunt. A proper chimp kiss is done with the mouth wide open, but she'd done hers human-style, though admittedly she'd produced more suck than she'd meant to. She settled against Mom's shoulder and without thinking lifted her hand and started to pick with inquisitive fingers among the roots of the gray-streaked hair. She felt Mom stiffen and then try to relax.

"You won't find anything, darling," she said.

The chimps in the Research Section of the Pool were allowed a few harmless parasites so that they could have the satisfaction of catching them in their endless grooming sessions, but a flake of dried skin or a scrap of dirt would do almost as well. That wasn't the point.

"Mm-hmmm," Eva murmured on a rising note.

Mom twitched and relaxed again.

"Don't tease," she said. "I'm not in the mood."

Eva shrugged her shoulder forward and said, "You do me. It's kind of comforting."

"All right. Provided you don't go poking in my earhole."

Eva peered at the dark cave in the neat whorled ear. Yes, she did feel a definite urge to probe in there with a finger, but it wouldn't be fair. Mom had never felt easy with the chimps, the way Eva had. She couldn't even groom a shoulder as though it was the natural thing to be doing; there was a sort of fumblingness about her fingertips as they worked their way across the fur. All the same, it was lovely to be able to feel the movement after the weeks of stillness and numbness. If she'd been a cat, Eva would have purred.

"I'm supposed to be talking to you," said Mom.

"Uh?"

"Have you thought about the sort of life you're going to live when you're up and about?"

"Lots. Skiing's going to be fun."

The snow peaks and the beaches were almost the only human playgrounds left. There wasn't a lot else you could do with them. Mom chuckled.

"My legs are going to be so strong," said Eva. "And I can get my center of gravity right down. I could be a world-beater. How'd you like to have a famous daughter?"

"Not much. People are going to be a bit interested in you anyway, darling. You know how they are about chimps as it is."

"They'll get used to me. Anyway, I want to be ordinary—go back to school, be with Bren and Ginny . . . They came around last night, you know?"

"They said they might . . . I'm afraid there's a little more to it than that, darling."

"Uh?"

"Haven't you wondered where the funds have come from for all this?"

Mom tilted her head to show she meant the room and the machines and the control room beyond and so on.

"Research, I guess."

"Of course, but research still has to be funded. Dad and I couldn't have afforded it, and the Pool's got nothing to spare. Joan may be famous, but she's still got to get her funds from somewhere. What she did, in fact, was set up a sort of arrangement with SMI—you know, the shaper people—and they raised the money from some of their advertisers who were interested. World Fruit's the main one, I believe."

"You mean I'm *sponsored*!"

Eva used the keyboard to make such a squeak of outrage that Mom laughed aloud.

"I'm afraid so, my darling. Public TV couldn't afford you."

"Grrgh!"

"And, of course, this means that SMI is going to want to do at least one program about you. There are other things, like World Fruit having an option for you to appear in some of the Honeybear commercials . . ."

"Uh?"

"They can't *make* you, if we don't agree, but you aren't

allowed to advertise anyone else's products—that's what an option means."

"Might be fun. And *lots* of grapes."

"Is that all you can think of? I'm trying to explain to you that quite soon SMI is going to start wanting to film you again. They did some while you were asleep, but Joan wouldn't let them since then because it might have . . . oh, it's too long to explain. Anyway, they're going to do this program and some more after, perhaps, and they've spent so much money on you that they're bound to want to make a production of it, and . . ."

"Do I have to?"

"Well, yes, at least one. That's in the contract. After that . . . You see, *if* people are interested in you, enough of them, then that's going to mean more programs, and that's going to mean money coming in, not just for you and Dad and me—I mean it'd be nice, but we don't really . . . You see, we actually *owe* Joan, morally I mean, for what she's done. Then there's the Pool . . ."

Mom sighed. The Pool was always desperate for funds. It was a fact that Eva had grown up with, almost like the law of gravity.

"Okay," she said. "If it's for the Pool."

"I knew you'd say that."

"Provided they don't try and make out I'm some kind of freak."

A pause. Mom sort of squaring her shoulders, inside.

"There's bound to be a bit of that, darling. I mean, we've got to get used to the idea that people are going to stare. Some people. I suppose in the long run it's going to be up to you to show them you're not."

In her skiing fantasy Eva had imagined the gawps of the other skiers as she careered down the slopes. And school—of course heads would turn when she first came into class, but kids get used to things pretty quickly. She hadn't really thought about living her life as the object of an endless stare. People!

No, you didn't have to have people, not all the time.

"Okay," she said. "And when it gets to be too much, I can always go and join the Pool and be a chimp for a while."

She felt Mom's body stiffen beneath her, as if she'd gotten a cramp. Eva thought she'd just been keeping the conversation going, but now . . . yes, better get it said. It was important.

"It's all right, Mom. I'll only go to the Reserve."

"Are you serious?"

"Mind you, if I went to a Public Section, people wouldn't know which one was me. I'd have to take my clothes off, of course."

"Please, darling . . ."

"It's all right, Mom."

"Let's talk about something else."

That was family code, just like a chimp code, only in words —a way of not getting into an argument. You chose another subject and hoped the argument would simply go away, like a headache—only this one, Eva knew, wasn't going to, but for now she obeyed the code.

"What about clothes, then?" she said.

"Yes, we've got to work that out. Have you got any ideas?"

"Bow in my hair?"

Mom managed a laugh. She'd always loved making clothes for her pretty daughter. The chimps in the Pool mostly wore nothing but were dressed in child's overalls when Dad took them on expeditions, partly because they weren't housebroken and had to use diapers, but mainly to hide the sexual swellings on the rumps of the females, which people who didn't know about chimps always found embarrassing.

"I'm a different shape now," said Eva.

"A challenge, darling. I'll bring my tape measure tomorrow."

"Nothing fancy, Mom. I hate it in the commercials when they put chimps into frills. Just overalls, mostly."

"I suppose so."

"I'm not going to try and look human."

Silence, but Eva could feel the sigh.

"It's important, Mom. I've got to be happy with this new me, and so do you. Not just think it's better than me being dead. Happy to have me like this."

"I'm trying, darling. I really am trying."

Poor Mom. It was much harder for her. When you're born you get imprinted with your mother's face, and she with yours. It happens with a lot of animals, some more strongly than others. With humans it's about middling, but the bond is still there, deep inside you, hard to alter. Eva still had the same Mom she'd always known, but Mom had this new thing, this stranger, this changeling. She couldn't help yearning in her depths for her own daughter, the one with the long black hair and blue eyes and the scar on her left earlobe where a chimp had bitten her when she was three. However much she taught herself to think of this new Eva as that daughter, it wasn't the same as feeling she was.

It was unfair to push her too hard. Eva stopped grooming Mom's hair and took her hand and held it, human-style. Mom squeezed back but let go. Eva's was not the hand she needed, not any longer. It was long and bony-fingered with hair on the back. How could anyone pretend it was her daughter's?

And, Eva knew, Mom was trying harder than anyone else would, ever.

MONTH TWO,
DAY TWENTY-FIVE

Awake.
Standing by the window, looking down, nerve ends
  electric . . .
Like standing on a cliff top, imagining falling . . .
Falling into the world, people, people, people . . .
Having to move among them, to begin to live . . .

"Big day," said Robbo.

Eva turned at the sound of his voice. He stood smiling at the door, handsome as a shaper cop. His skin glistened like a fresh nut. He was wearing a brand-new outfit, straight from the store, with fawn trousers molded to his legs and a loose fawn jacket above. He'd had his hair styled and his mustache trimmed. It was a big day for everyone.

"I like the butterfly," he said.

"Mom couldn't resist it."

It was gold-and-purple, stitched on to the left pocket of Eva's new green overalls. She liked it too.

"Let's see you walk, then . . . You call that walking?"

"You want me to do *tricks*?"

She didn't get the sneer quite right. Practicing when you were alone wasn't the same as talking, and she still made mistakes. Robbo was used to it and hardly noticed, but from today on it mattered. People judge other people by their voices. If you sound stupid, you are stupid. If you don't sound real, you aren't—you're not a person.

"I've seen chimps walking," said Robbo. "Of their own accord."

"When they've got something to carry. Like I've seen humans crawling."

"Okay, okay, walk how you want. Let's go and look at this gym, huh? They've just about gotten it finished in time."

He turned and held the door for Eva as if going through it was the most ordinary thing you could think of. Last evening, while Dad and Joan and Ali and Meg and the rest of the team had stood around, Dr. Richter had ceremonially removed the last pair of sensor cables that tied her to the machines. Champagne corks had popped. Everyone had wished her good luck. And today she was free. Going through the door was like being hatched, coming out of her safe egg into the huge world.

The world was a shambles. First there was a little empty vestibule and beyond that the control room, where new machines were being uncrated; technicians were arguing over a wiring diagram; a supervisor was frowning at a printout. Eva knuckled through the mess beside Robbo and out into a wide hospital corridor. She was glad now of the boring exercises he and the physios had made her do all the last seven weeks. She felt none of the tiredness and heaviness you'd have expected after all that time in bed—in fact, an exhilarating lightness filled her, becoming stronger and stronger until she lost control and went scampering on ahead, hooting with pleasure as she ran.

Then she stopped dead, with all the hairs along her back prickling erect. Her call had been answered, not with the same call but with a series of short breathy barks on a slightly rising note snapped off into silence. A chimp call. Eva had never heard it before, but she knew, or rather she felt, what it meant. *Alone*, it said. *Lost. Frightened. Where are you?* She felt the answer rising in her throat but suppressed it as Robbo caught up with her.

"Who's that?" she said.

"Who's what?"

The call began again while Eva was still pressing keys. *Alone. Lost* . . .

"That, you mean?" said Robbo. "Next patient, I guess. Now that Prof. Pradesh has proved she can do it with you . . ."

"They're going to do *lots*?" Kelly after Kelly after Kelly?

Eva stayed where she was, her pelt crawling at the thought. Robbo was already moving on and glanced back at her, puzzled.

"Sure. Got to try again, don't they? Check it all out? That's how science works. You want to be the only one?"

Eva grunted and knuckled on beside him down the corridor. She didn't know what she wanted. Anyway, they couldn't do lots—there weren't enough chimps. But Robbo was right— they'd do some, as many as they could probably. Not to save lives either, though that would come into it, but the real reason was in the human mind. It couldn't stop asking, the human mind. Once it found one thing out, it had to move on. And *then* what? it kept saying. You do one experiment and it works, so you try it again, with a difference, to see if that works too. And again and again . . . So there wasn't just one chimp shut up, lonely, frightened, bewildered, having its blood sampled, its brain rhythms measured, all that. Eva's control room was having new gadgets moved in so it could take care of more than one experiment . . .

"Now, what do you think of that!"

"Hoo!"

"Who, *what*?"

"Okay, who paid for it?"

"You can't read?"

Eva looked again. The gym wasn't large, but it shone like a glossy new toy and smelled of fresh plastic and varnish. In one corner a shaper crew was rigging lights and a camera. There was a climbing frame, a trapeze, a vaulting horse, and a lot of moveable stuff; and every item, she now saw, had the Honeybear logo on it. Eva knew it so well that she hadn't noticed it. Because Honeybear used chimps in its commercials there'd always been free Honeybear drinks at home, ever since she could remember. Now there was a free gym. Okay.

She knuckled across the floor and swung herself up into the frame.

"Hey! Take it easy!" said Robbo. "Don't want you breaking a rib. We should've had a week at least, trying out what you can do before they did the program. Watch it!"

Impossible to obey. It was so glorious to be moving like this, reaching, grasping, swinging across. She knew she was still only about half strong, despite the exercises—when she was fully fit a grown man would have trouble holding her—but now what mattered was the sheer pleasure of movement, the feeling of naturalness. This was what these arms, these fingers, were for. It mattered because it allowed her to understand the rightness of this new body, to feel its beauty and energy . . .

"Watch it, I said!" snapped Robbo.

Eva squatted into a crook of the frame and hooted derisively, but in fact he'd been right. For a moment, quite unpredictably, the ghost of a human arm had flickered into her mind, making her miss her grip, forcing her to grab with the other hand, clutch. The ghost came back even more strongly when she tried to swing. Long ago, as a small girl, that body had learned the to-and-fro rhythm, the exact timing needed to fling her weight on the chains and drive the swing forward through its arc. This body was differently weighted. Its arms were the wrong length. The rhythm wouldn't come. Thinking didn't help, because the old human timing was imprinted below the level of thought, putting a jiggle into the arc and spoiling the acceleration. Swinging was something she'd have to learn fresh.

What about riding a bike? There was a kid's bike with fat tires and the Honeybear logo freshly painted on its side, but there wasn't room to use it in the gym, with the mess of cables cluttering the floor, so she took it out into the corridor to try. Balancing turned out to be easy, and she could grip the pedals with her feet, but her legs didn't understand about moving in circles. She was wobbling along, concentrating on the pedal movement when some people came out of a door just ahead of her, not looking where they were going, because the man in front was talking over his shoulder. Trying to miss him, Eva steered into the wall and crashed. That stopped their talk.

She picked herself up and saw that the man she'd missed was a stranger, though there was something familiar about him all the same. If he hadn't been wearing heavy dark glasses she might have recognized him. The people he'd been talking to over his shoulder were Dad and Joan Pradesh and a nervous-looking young woman. Eva rippled her fingers over the keys.

"Hi, Dad. Got to learn all over fresh."

"Better learn to look where you're going."

"This is her?" said the stranger.

"This is Eva," said Joan. "This is Dirk Ellan, Eva. I'm sure you've seen him on the shaper."

Eva grunted a greeting. The man just nodded, not to her but to Joan, telling her Yes, he'd seen this chimp. Something about the nod made the name click. Dirk Ellan! Of course, though Eva hadn't watched his programs often. Dad had taught her to be scornful of the sort of predigested science you got on the shaper.

"We were coming to see how you were getting along," said Dad.

"She's been doing fine, Dr. Adamson," said Robbo. "Times

you wouldn't know she wasn't a chimp. Few things she can't handle yet."

"Like riding a bike," said Dad.

He was smiling inside his beard. Too much. Eva wasn't surprised at the way Robbo had hurried to get his word in, but Dad! All anxious and eager. And Mr. Ellan's nods and silences showed that he was used to this sort of reaction—expected it, in fact. It was just like the chimps in the Pool, with their boss males, and the other males constantly making special signals to placate or challenge the bosses. Eva didn't remember noticing humans behaving like this in the old days, but now everything the three men did seemed obvious, a language she'd always known.

Back in the gym she climbed and swung a bit to show them what she could do. Then there was a long wait while the shaper people set the cameras up and discussed angles and changed their minds and argued. Then she went through her paces; first, things chimps could do naturally, like climbing and swinging; then things they might be taught to do, like riding a bike; and then things they couldn't, like building a self-supporting arch of toy bricks. There were long waits between each take.

Eva needed the rests. She was still only half strong and tired quickly. So she sat hunkered into a fork of the climbing frame and watched the others, Dad trying to impress Mr. Ellan, Joan ignoring the hustle and working at some problem on scraps of paper, Robbo chatting up one of the shaper women. Sometimes a sort of irritation swelled up inside her, making her pelt bristle, urging her to go swinging wildly around the frame, barking as she went. Mostly she suppressed it, but at one moment, noticing a camera trained on her as though she were some kind of *thing* you didn't have to say Do-you-mind to, she stretched her lips forward without thinking and gave it a Go-away hoot. The whole group turned and stared. As startled as they were, Eva shrugged, grinned, and waved a hand. Forget it. They forgot it and went on with what they'd been doing.

When she'd done enough tricks to keep them happy, Mr. Ellan came over and leaned against the frame beside Eva. His whole personality changed as the cameras closed around the pair of them. He'd taken his dark glasses off, letting the world see the smile lines crinkling at the corners of his eyes. He was relaxed, friendly, trustworthy, understanding—all that. Eva knew it was just his job, a performance, but all the same she felt her skin unprickle.

"So you're Eva?" he said.

"And you're Dirk Ellan."

"Right. I better explain to viewers there's got to be that little blip while that gizmo you've got puts the words together for you. And just in case there's some real meanies out there, thinking it's all a trick, how about you spelling out something real slow, so we can show 'em it just ain't so?"

Eva grunted, eased the keyboard from its loops, and held it so that a camera could watch while with one thin dark finger she pressed the individual keys.

"You've got it wrong, you meanies."

She rewound the little tape and played the words several times, varying the tone of voice.

"That's amazing," said Mr. Ellan. Eva thought she could just hear a flicker of real surprise under the easy public accent. Perhaps he'd been wondering too—why not? Anyway, he was a meanie himself, in spite of the signals. Deliberately she gave him a genuine chimp snicker. His eyebrows went up.

"But inside there you're really a young woman?" he said.

"I'm Eva, okay."

He didn't seem to notice her answer wasn't the same as Yes. He wouldn't.

"And how exactly does it feel?"

Eva managed to suppress another snicker. This was one of Dad's bugbears—"and how *exactly* does it feel, Mrs. Hrumph, to have your husband reveal he's a practicing werewolf?"—but she'd promised herself she was going to be on her best behavior. The program was important for everyone, especially the Pool. The trouble was that Mr. Ellan filled her with a spirit of mischief—and *that* wouldn't have been there in the old days either.

"It feels great," she said. "I'm looking forward to things."

"No regrets?"

"No regrets."

"I've seen pictures of you. You used to be a very pretty little miss. How about that?"

Eva glanced a him. He was horrible. Didn't he realize Mom would be watching? She wanted to bite his ear off. No. But she'd get him somehow.

"I'm very pretty now," she said.

"Sure, but . . ."

"Don't you think so?"

"Like I say . . ."

Deliberately she reached out, gripped the immaculate collar and hauled him toward her. He yelled. She heard a shout of "Eva!" from Dad, but by then she was giving Mr. Ellan a kiss, not a proper open-mouthed chimp kiss but using her big lips to produce a real smacker, maximum vacuum. He was still trying to push her clear when she let go. He backed off while she sat laughing in the nook of the frame. He managed a sort of laugh too, but she could see the fright and fury in his eyes, just as she could feel the various reactions from the dimness beyond the camera lights, pleasure and alarm and excitement all mixed together. The shaper people, they must know he was a meanie. By the sound of their laughter, they did.

"Gee, you're strong," he said.

"Chimps are."

"But you're supposed to be a young woman."

"I'm a chimp too. And I like it."

"Sure, sure."

PART TWO
LIVING

MONTH FOUR, DAY TWELVE

Living at home, at last . . .
But the ghost still there . . .
The ghost moving about these rooms . . .
Making herself snacks in this kitchen . . .
Gazing, now, out this window . . .

There was a particular moment sometimes when the sun went down. It needed the right weather, a cloudless sky and a mild west wind to clear the brownish haze of the city. Then for a few moments, below the earliest stars and above the still-faint pattern of city lights, you might just catch a different kind of glimmer, a wavering thread, the twinkle of snow on mountain peaks, ninety kilometers off, catching the sun's last rays.

Eva watched for it, and yes, it was there, but the old prickle of pleasure didn't come. Her happiest times used to be skiing. She would look forward for months to her next chance. But now it was only the ghost that yearned.

The ghost had been particularly strong this morning, because of being home and waking in her own bed. Eva had awakened on the edge of horrors, desperate for the feel of her own long-limbed smooth-skinned body, her own hair to brush, her own teeth to clean, her own dark blue eyes to ring with eye shadow. Dad had had to give her an extra shot of dope she still took to suppress that kind of feeling, so perhaps that was why the ghost that yearned for the ski slopes was now only a vague shadow in her mind, and Eva, the new Eva, the one she must learn to think and feel of as the only real

Eva, was merely amused and interested in the idea of going skiing. She might have been excited if Dad had announced they were going off to the mountains next weekend, but she didn't yearn anymore. That kind of intense, shapeless longing was for something else.

What?

The answer came when she closed her eyes. Leaves mottling the dark behind the eyelids. Trees. Only where could you still find trees, real trees in forests, the way you could still find mountains?

Up north in the timber stands, grown as a thirty-year crop? No good. The branches were the wrong shape to swing through or nest among. You couldn't live through those winters. You couldn't eat pine needles. South, then? There were bits of jungle still—you saw them sometimes on the shaper. Nearly three thousand kilometers on beyond the mountains, there were five or six valleys that had never been cleared, where the rain-forest trees still grew and the lianas dangled. There were a few other places in the world like that, tiny preserved patches, most of them funded by the shaper companies, studied and guarded by scientists, kept free from other human intrusion. But perhaps Dad might be able to arrange something, a research project which needed a sort-of-chimp to be in a jungle for a while . . .

It was a fantasy, and Eva knew it. It was a way of dreaming the dream. She kept her eyes closed and let it happen. Unnoticed beside her the ghost thinned, dwindled, vanished.

Beep. Beep. Beep. Mom had no sense of time, so she set the kitchen timer for anything that mattered. Its shrill sound stopped and Mom came into the living room and switched on the shaper. A travel commercial filled the zone, bronze bodies on a pale beach, ridiculously less crowded than a real beach would be. Mom settled into her chair and Eva knuckled over and climbed into her lap. Mom laughed resignedly.

"I suppose we've got to watch," she said.

"Dad's big day."

Eva was glad she'd made enough fuss to force them to let her come home in time to watch the program with Mom. It wouldn't have been fair to Mom to make her watch it alone. Dad was down at the studios because part of the format of Mr. Ellan's programs was always a live discussion. Mom could have come to the hospital to watch, of course, but that would have been making too big a thing of it. Much better here at home, ordinary.

When the titles began Mom turned up the sound, and the drumbeat theme of the series thudded out. The zone cleared, and then filled with a section of ice rink, a girl with long black hair skating in a yellow tracksuit. Her slightly fuzzy edges showed that the sequence had been taken with an amateur camera. Mom stiffened and closed her eyes. Mr. Ellan's solemn half whisper began as a voice-over.

"This girl's name is Eva. Just over a year ago she was involved in a car accident and suffered extensive physical damage. She would certainly never have walked, let alone skated, again. Furthermore, she was in an irreversible coma. Yet today Eva is alive, active, healthy. She looks, however, quite different. She looks like *this*."

And there was Kelly, squatting among the yellow bars of the climbing frame. She pursed her lips forward and hooted. *Go away*—but to humans it would be just a hoot, and anyway she immediately shrugged, grinned, and waved a friendly hand. Eva stared. Me, she thought. Me. Though she was used by now to looking at her own image in a mirror and accepting it as herself, the chimp in the zone was like a stranger. The brown eyes were bright with cleverness and mischief. The big ears stuck out through the coarse black hair. Eva felt a rush of friendliness and liking, and without thinking started a silent pant of greeting. Faintly she was aware of the old Eva gazing through her eyes, dismayed, trying to make the lips and throat cry *No!*, but thanks to the dope it wasn't difficult to blank her out and will a *Yes* with her conscious mind. She glanced up, wanting to share that *Yes*. Mom still had her eyes shut.

"Try and watch, Mom," she made the keyboard murmur. "It's me now. We've got to like this me. I do already. Really. I'm not pretending."

"I'm so glad, darling."

"I know it's harder for you."

"I'll learn."

The climbing frame vanished, leaving Kelly hanging in mid-air as a still. The girl in the yellow tracksuit appeared on the opposite side of the zone, and Mr. Ellan strolled up between them as though he'd just happened along.

"In the next hour," he said, "we are going to show you the full story of this astonishing event. Before we begin I should point out that but for the generosity of Honeybear Soft Drinks it would not have been possible. Eva's transformation was a very expensive procedure, demanding the attention of many highly skilled scientists working at the very frontier of technology. Such work does not come cheap, and Eva and her parents have cause to be very grateful indeed to Honeybear for its help. We have with us in the studio this evening one of those parents, Dr. Daniel Adamson of the International Chimpanzee Pool . . ."

The zone widened and there was Dad, smiling at the cameras, his blue eyes bright in the studio lights, his whole face and attitude saying *Like me, oh, please like me.*

". . . and we are also honored to have with us Professor Joan Pradesh, whose work in the field of neuron memory, first discovered by her father, Professor E. K. Pradesh, made the miracle of Eva possible . . ."

And there was Joan. Somebody had bullied her into wearing a mauve dress. She didn't even bother to smile.

". . . Now, first, Dr. Adamson, perhaps you can tell us how exactly you and your wife felt . . ."

"I can't listen to this," said Mom and switched the sound off. "You've got it taping for Dad, haven't you?"

Eva grunted a yes. She didn't mind—she could listen later too. And meanwhile it was interesting to watch Dad trying to tell Mr. Ellan how *exactly* . . . And then there was a picture of Dad's car lying upside down with its roof caved in; and then a shape on a hospital bed, a mound of bandages with tubes running in and out—Mom had her eyes shut again—and then the same shape, with a sort of box like a coffin beside it. The cameras closed in to a little window in the lid of the box. Dimly, behind the glass, you could see something that might have been a dark, furry head with its eyes closed . . .

Eva was glad they had the sound off. There was something holy about the silent pair, something you didn't want Mr. Ellan, or even Dad, telling you what to think about . . . But it was interesting that they'd started making the program even then, so that Honeybear could have something to pay for. It must all have cost a fortune, Eva realized. They'd be wanting to see returns on their money from now on.

"It's all right, you can look now. It's Joan," she said, switching up the sound.

Joan was pure Joan, despite the mauve dress, looking and sounding as if she thought the program was a complete waste of her time. She didn't even try to make things easier for the dimwits out there watching, but Mr. Ellan was pretty good at his job, really, asking his questions in a way that forced her to give the dimwits a chance. They'd only been going a few minutes when the commo beeped. Mom picked it up with her free hand.

"Hello. Who? Oh, no. No, I don't want to talk about it. No thank you."

She hung up.

"A woman from some other program," she said. "How did they get our new number? It isn't on the . . ."

The commo beeped again. She picked it up, said hello, listened for a moment, and hung up. Eva reached over and switched it to autocall.

". . . that Eva was used to chimps?" Mr. Ellan was saying. "From what Dr. Adamson was telling us, she'd practically grown up with them."

The zone showed another amateur sequence, a naked human child with blue eyes and dark hair absorbed in play in a sandbox. A half-grown female chimp knuckled into view and started to search intently across her scalp. The child seemed hardly to notice.

"I can only say it *may* have been of importance," Joan said. "The brain is an extremely complex mechanism, and we do not yet understand many things about it. In this case, the problems of rejection in the immediately posttransferral stage may well have been eased by experiences analogous to maternal imprinting in Eva's early childhood. However . . ."

The doorbell rang. One of the neighbors, thought Eva, checking to see if we know the program's on—people can be thick—they couldn't use the commo because we're on auto. She was moving to tell them Thanks, we're watching, when Mom said "Wait," turned the volume down, and switched the shaper to closed circuit. The zone filled with the landing outside the apartment door. Four people stood there, two of them with shaper cameras and the other two jostling to hold up their ID cards to the closed-circuit camera above the lintel. They were calling out something, inaudibly because the volume was off. Behind them the elevator doors opened and more people jostled out, some with cameras.

"I knew this was going to happen," said Mom. "Jerry swore he wouldn't let anyone through the main doors, but I just knew."

"How'd they get here so soon?" said Eva. "I thought . . ."

"SMI did a lot of publicity. They guaranteed no one would be told our name in advance, but somebody at the studios must have sold it to the other companies. Shaper people will do *anything*."

The doorbell was ringing now without stopping. People were banging at the door itself. It was supposed to be break-in–proof, but you couldn't be sure. Mom pressed a couple of keys and spoke into the mouthpiece of her control.

"This is Mrs. Adamson. We are not giving any interviews. Will you please go away? You are trespassing on private property."

Nothing happened. Perhaps they hadn't heard through the racket they were making, hammering and calling and swearing at one another and pressing the bell. Even from right inside the apartment the noise was loud enough to feel dangerous. More people came out of the elevator. Mom repeated her message. And again and again. The doorbell stopped. Now they were shouting at one another not to shout at one another, and making shushing gestures. Then silence. You could see they could hear the message because half a dozen microphones poked up toward the speaker to record Mom's voice. It didn't do any good. The bell started again at once, and the shouting and knocking.

Now the door on the other side of the landing opened, and little Mr. Koo came out to complain about the racket. The Koos never watched the shaper, so he couldn't have understood what was happening, but the moment they saw him the reporters closed around him like wasps attacking a caterpillar, yelling questions and thrusting microphones and cameras at him. He retreated, but before he could close the door they surged in around him, leaving room on the landing for the elevator to disgorge another load, and these newcomers, seeing their rivals streaming through an open door, must have thought the Adamsons lived on that side and pressed in after them while the poor old elevator went down for yet another load.

White and shuddering, Mom plugged the commo in. It immediately started to bleep, but after several tries she hit a clear space and got a channel out. She called the police, but whoever she spoke to said they couldn't help. Then she tried the home number of a man she knew in the police department, because of her job, and he said the same, explaining privately that the police never interfered with shaper people if they could help it, because the shaper people always got their own back by putting on programs that made that department look like crooks or idiots.

The moment she put it down the commo began to beep again, till she switched to auto. The doorbell was getting on Eva's nerves, so she went out into the hallway to see if she could turn it off. The sound came from a box up by the ceiling. She opened the door of the coat closet, jumped, grasped, and swung herself up. Crouching on top of the door, clutching it with her feet, she inspected the box. There wasn't a switch, but there was a grill in front through which the sound came, so she swung down and got a box of rice from the kitchen. Using the lid of the box as a sort of chute, she eased a stream of rice into the grill until the noise stopped.

She didn't come down at once. She felt safer crouched up there away from the floor. The voices from beyond the door made her pelt prickle, and her throat and lips worked involuntarily, wanting to shout back. Though she couldn't hear any words, the voices still had a meaning—they were hunting cries, the calls of a pack baying outside the lair of its prey. Of course, if they'd been let in the people out there wouldn't have hurt her, only asked stupid questions. That was what her mind told her. But her body told her they were enemy. It was an effort to climb down and go back into the living room.

Mom was still white and shivering.

"Hadn't we better call Dad?" said Eva, using the tone control on her keyboard to sound calm.

"The program's still on. He'll be at the studio."

"You better warn him. He'll never get in."

Again it took several tries to get a channel out, but in the end Mom managed to find someone who said they'd tell Dad as soon as they could.

"I never dreamed it would be as bad as this," said Mom. "I realized they'd be interested, but honestly! They're mad!"

No, they're just people, thought Eva. Time went by. The riot on the landing calmed. The onslaught became a siege. Some of the attackers settled onto the floor and waited; others leaned against walls; a few spoke into pocket commos.

"Let's watch something else," said Eva, taking the control and beginning to flick through the channels. The second one she came to was showing an old tape of chimps. She watched for a while until she realized from the voice-over that it was a news program about her, only they didn't have anything to show the viewers except that tape. Three channels farther on she found another news program, live, with a reporter talking into a camera in the street outside this very apartment house. Almost at once the shot switched to another angle from far higher, this building still, against the evening sky, with the city spreading on beyond it until it was lost in its own manmade dusky mist. The focus zoomed in to a particular window. The lights were on in the room, so you could just make out a woman sitting in a chair, with a large dark something on her lap.

Mom sighed and pressed keys to lower the blind. In the imaged window in the zone the blind came down.

"Someone in one of the other buildings must have let them use their apartment," said Mom. "Honestly, people will do *anything.*"

People, people, people—even Mom talked as if they were enemy, and she was people too. She switched the shaper off, just leaving the VCR running so that Dad could watch his big moment tomorrow.

More than an hour later they were halfheartedly playing chess when Eva felt her pelt prickle with wariness. Something had changed. Though she hadn't been aware of hearing the crowd on the landing, now that she listened for them she knew that they had stopped muttering among themselves and become very quiet. She switched the closed circuit on and saw that they were all standing up, facing the elevator. She could hear the whine of its ascent.

"Dad," said Mom. "But he'll . . . how did they know?"

They had friends with commos below, of course, thought Eva, but she didn't have time to say so before the elevator stopped and the door opened. Two huge men in gray uniforms faced the crowd, which had begun to surge forward. They lowered their shoulders and charged out. Now Eva could see that there were four other people in the elevator, Dad, a woman, and two more huge men in uniform. The crowd gave way before the charge but then surged in from the side as the second two guards tried to hustle Dad and the woman on through the gap. Dad looked terrified, though often you could hardly see him for outthrust microphones. The woman held herself very erect and spoke in a loud voice, clearly saying the same few words over and over. The guards elbow-jabbed the crowd aside. Eva saw at least one bleeding nose, and several people fell right over. When they reached the door the guards regrouped and kept the crowd at bay while Dad bent down to operate the voice lock, but either because of the racket or because he was so scared his voice came out funny and the lock didn't work at once, so Eva got there first and opened the door.

The crowd could barely have glimpsed her, but they let out

a baying roar and surged forward as Dad and the woman slipped through. The guards just managed to hold them while Eva got the door shut.

Dad stood in the hall, shaking his head while the baying dwindled into shouts of pleading and frustration. He scuffed his toe at some of the rice Eva had spilled while she was silencing the bell.

"I didn't believe it," he said. "I just didn't believe it."

"It is certainly far worse than anyone had expected," said the woman, as calm as if she were discussing the weather. She was a bit over thirty, blond, with fluffy hair and neat features. At first glance she looked rather fragile, despite her dark business suit, but she spoke and carried herself as though she weren't afraid of anyone. She turned to Mom, who had come out into the hallway.

"Good evening, Mrs. Adamson. I am Jane Callaway, from the legal and contract department of SMI. Before anything else, I must apologize on behalf of the company for the intolerable disturbance you have suffered tonight."

"It's awful," said Mom.

"Let's have a drink," said Dad.

"Just fruit juice for me," said Ms. Callaway. "I'm working."

Eva knuckled into the kitchen and got the drinks, making Dad's a bit stronger than usual. Ms. Callaway said Thank you in a perfectly normal way but then sat looking at Eva with cool, considering pale eyes.

"I wish I'd seen her sooner," she said. "I think I might have realized. It may all die down in a few days, but in my opinion you are going to have to prepare for quite a long period of very intense media interest. That is why I'm here. My job is to work out the problems that arise in cases like this."

"There can't be many cases like this!" said Mom.

"There are always unique features," said Ms. Callaway. "That's why the public is interested. But the legal basis remains remarkably constant. In my experience, your most straightforward course would be to assign exclusive rights to Eva's story to a company such as SMI. Part of the contract would be that we protect you from unwanted intrusion. As a private citizen you can't sue a reporter who tries to question you, but we can, because the reporter is asking you to break your contract with us. Now obviously you don't want to embark on a long-term contract without thinking it over, but in view of what has happened it would be a sensible course for you to assign the rights to the story in the next few days . . ."

She had opened her briefcase while she was speaking and pulled out a few sheets of paper. She continued to explain, cool, friendly, helpful. Eva stopped listening. There was something about the three of them—Mom and Dad and Ms. Callaway—that puzzled her. Mom was frowning, Dad leaning forward in his chair, bright-eyed, nodding at each fresh point Ms. Callaway made . . . This wasn't his sort of thing at all, but Mom though she wasn't a lawyer knew a lot about things like contracts, because her job often involved trying to help people who'd gotten into some kind of legal mess . . . Why was Dad so anxious? Why wasn't he trying to get his word in, as usual? Was it just that he was tired after the program and still shocked by what had happened on the landing? Or . . .

Out of nowhere the thought floated into Eva's mind that Dad was acting. He already knew what Ms. Callaway was going to say. He'd already talked to her about all this. And that meant . . .

No, he couldn't have known it was going to be like this. He hadn't been acting when he got home. He'd been really frightened, really shocked . . . But suppose Ms. Callaway's company *had* realized what was going to happen. Suppose they just allowed it to happen in cases like this and then sent someone like Ms. Callaway along, cool, friendly, helpful, while

you had the reporter-pack actually baying on your doormat
and all you could think of was getting rid of them. What
they'd do was calm Dad down and get him to sort-of-agree not
to worry till the time came, and tell him about the long-term
contract and the kind of money that would be coming to the
Pool, and he'd have sort-of-agreed to that too, and then sort-
of-told them about Mom and how she might react to the idea
of assigning exclusive rights to her daughter's story to a shaper
company . . .

Slowly Eva tapped a few words into her keyboard and
waited for a pause before she pressed the "Speak" bar.

"Do you know who I belong to?"

The three heads jerked around.

"You don't belong to anyone, darling," said Mom.

Dad said nothing but looked at Ms. Callaway. She stared at
Eva and nodded, like a teacher when someone's asked the
right question.

"As a matter of fact, that is a very interesting point," she
said. "I have, of course been looking into it."

"Why?" said Mom, sharply.

"Because I am paid to be sure of our legal ground before we
undertake long-term commitments. I believe that when animals from the Chimpanzee Pool are sold for research they are
sold outright, and the organization doing the research then
buys them. But in Eva's case, because the experiment was
carried out by the Pool itself, in cooperation with the Pradesh
Institute, no such arrangement was made—in fact, no arrangement was made at all."

"I suppose I ought . . ." said Dad.

"There might therefore be an argument that Eva's body, at
least, still belongs to the Pool."

"This is ridiculous," said Mom. "Anyway, we could pay for
her now—we'd have to find the money somehow."

"The difficulty, Mrs. Adamson, is that Eva is now an extremely valuable piece of property. The trustees of the Pool might well argue . . ."

"She isn't property!"

"Well, I would agree that if the case were to go to court, Eva could eventually be confirmed as a human being—that is to say not belonging to anyone, but with her parents having the usual rights and responsibilities while she remains a minor. Even a point like that raises problems. How old is she? The human Eva is thirteen, but the body she is using is less than six. All I can tell you is that however the courts decide these points, the legal costs in coming to a decision might well prove very considerable indeed. That is why I have drafted a special clause into this contract under which my company accepts that Eva is fully human, with all that that implies, and furthermore, the company undertakes, in the event of your signing a long-term contract with us, to bear all legal costs in arguing the case."

"You got this all ready beforehand?" said Mom.

Ms. Callaway smiled, unruffled.

"It's my job to think of difficulties before they happen. The short-term preliminary contract I suggest is only one option. If you would like to discuss . . ."

"No. Let's have a look at it."

Ms. Callaway passed the papers across. Mom put on her glasses and started to read. Dad beckoned to Eva. She knuckled across, climbed onto his lap, and started to finger through his beard.

"How did it go?" he muttered.

"Didn't have time to watch much. Joan had just started. Then *they* turned up."

She shrugged a shoulder toward the doorway.

"But you've got it on tape?"

"Uh."

They waited. Dad finished his drink. Ms. Callaway sat still, patient as a hunter. At last Mom looked up.

"I suppose that's the best course," she said. "You really think you can get rid of them?"

"It has usually worked in the past," said Ms. Callaway, calm as ever—but then for the first time she gave a small jerk of surprise as Mom turned to Eva.

"Listen, darling. If Dad and I sign this, it means that for the next week we agree not to talk about you to anyone except Ms. Callaway's company. We don't *have* to talk to them either if we don't want to during that week. But it means that they will have the legal right to shoo everyone else away, and that will give us all time to think. Are you happy about that?"

They had to wait while Eva thought and then, more slowly than usual, set her message up. She made the words come slowly too.

"All right. Only provided you don't sign anything saying ordinary chimps belong to people either."

She felt Dad's body jerk. Then he laughed his infuriating little laugh that meant that what you'd just said was too silly to argue about.

"I don't think there's anything . . ." murmured Mom.

"No," said Ms. Callaway, "and I will make a note to avoid phrases to that effect in future contracts. Now, if you will just sign here . . . and here, Dr. Adamson . . . excellent. And now I will see what I can do about driving the wolves from your door."

She stood up, patted her hair smooth, and left. The racket from the landing rose as the door opened, then faded. Mom switched on the closed circuit to watch but kept the volume off. Ms. Callaway, flanked by security men, was reading a statement—she must have had that ready too. The camera showed only the back of her head. Microphones jutted toward her. The crowd was listening. Their faces signaled weariness, frustration, defeat. Some at the back were talking into commos. The elevator doors were opening, and several of the crowd were already waiting to board it. When Ms. Callaway stopped reading, some questions were shouted, but she answered with a shake of her head. The elevator went down, crammed. Ms. Callaway came back into the apartment and talked to Mom and Dad about an appointment to which they could bring their own lawyer. By the time she left, the landing was almost empty, and the guards were shoving the last few reporters into the elevator by force. Two of the guards stayed on in case anyone tried to come back.

Eva awoke several times in the night. She was oddly restless in her own bed. In the old days she used to sleep on her stomach, stretched right out, but now she felt more comfortable curled up. I'd really like a basket, she thought, a big dog-basket, like a nest. I wonder if Mom would mind. Perhaps if I told her I wanted a round patchwork, to cover it with . . .

Later she woke again and heard voices, Mom and Dad, Mom angry and hurt, Dad trying to talk his way out. They both hated fights, didn't even like arguments, Dad especially. It was typical he hadn't ever figured out who owned Kelly, because that would have meant hassle. I'm going to have to watch Dad, Eva thought. Whatever he says, I'm going to see that I own me . . .

Another voice in the early dawn, only a murmur again but unmistakable. Mr. Ellan. Creeping out into the living room she found Dad settling down to watch his big moment. Since she'd missed so much with Mom turning the sound off and then the siege starting, she climbed onto his lap to watch too. He welcomed her by ruffling the fur at the back of her head with easy fingers.

Dad came over well on the shaper. In fact, Eva thought, he seemed more real than he sometimes did at home—sincere, solemn, and honest when he was talking about what had happened to his daughter, and then when he was talking about his chimps still sincere, but clever, excited, eager to make people understand. Now she could actually feel him purring with satisfaction at his own performance.

They watched the program through to the end. It finished with a kiss. When Eva had grabbed Mr. Ellan by the collar and given him that mighty, sucking smacker, some cameraman had had the wits to zoom right in and get it in close-up. No professional comic could have reacted quite as beautifully as Mr. Ellan did, his horrible self-satisfied calm suddenly ripped away, leaving him with bulging eyes, head uselessly twisted aside, mouth gaping in a yell of fright. Eva hugged herself. Dad laughed his big cheerful bay, which only came when he was genuinely amused.

The zone froze on the kiss, and the credits spun through. That meant they'd cut what Eva had said about being a chimp. Too bad, she thought. People had better start understanding that, or they wouldn't understand anything.

MONTH SIX, DAY TWO

Living with fame . . .

*Studios, waiting for programs to begin. Glare of shaper
   lights. How-exactly-does-it-feel . . .*

Autographs (no good chimp-grip for a pen). Stares. Giggles.

Money and treats and meeting shaper stars.

*A bodyguard, Cormac, in case you got kidnapped. A
   secretary, Joe, to answer the commo and the mail—
   journalists calling for a quick quote on Miss World or
   some diet fad, scientists wanting a slice of you (yes, a
   real slice sometimes, cells to culture, but usually only a
   slice of time and publicity) . . .*

Dad getting offered visiting professorships . . .

People, people, people . . .

As many grapes as you could eat . . .

Not enough time with Mom . . .

Partly it was Eva's own fault. She would have been stuck with
a little fame whatever she'd done. The people at SMI said that
long before the program was over, the Public Response Indica-
tors were already registering high interest and excitement.
That was why the reporters had been ringing at the door so
soon. But if only she'd never kissed Mr. Ellan. The PRI Index
had really hit the roof then, they said. That's what the billions of watchers had really gone for. Things that happened in
their shaper zones were more solid to them, more important,
more exciting than anything that happened in their own lives,
and somehow that image—the chimp squatting among the

yellow bars of the climbing frame, with the bright butterfly embroidered on her chest, and her glossy pelt and clear gaze, and then the great Dirk Ellan panicking in her grip, and the comic, huge-lipped kiss—people could never get enough of it. They had laughed and fallen in love. The sequence was played again and again and copied and parodied and referred to like a proverb everybody knew. On talk shows Eva had to cope with people trying to work themselves into a kiss-me position so that they could share the effect. All the crammed world, even oddballs like the Koos who never watched the shaper, knew about Eva.

Fame could be useful. Mom and the school social worker, who'd been around several times to talk things over before Eva started school again, had been worried about how the other kids would react—whispers, giggles, stares, outright re-jection perhaps. Eva herself had been pretty nervous the first day, but in fact there was hardly any of that at all. She found she wasn't a stranger. The kids felt they already knew her, seeing her so often on the shaper in their own homes. Some of the smaller ones were into a craze for imitating her voice, fluttering their fingers across imaginary keyboards on their chests and then speaking; some of them were so good Eva couldn't tell the difference. In most ways too, kids were more sensible about fame than adults. The stares and the auto-graphs lasted about two weeks, only. A few of the little ones hung around longer, not because she was famous—not even thinking about that—but because they felt a need to touch and fondle and be happy with a furry creature. Left to herself, Eva would probably have let it happen, but Ginny didn't like it and shooed the kids off.

Of course, there'd been hours of talk about all this at home. Mom had had the main teachers around and they'd discussed everything they could think of, from security against kidnappers to having a special small desk, but still there'd been things they'd missed . . .

Eva was sitting hunkered on the low wall in the shade of the Language Building with Bren beside her and Ginny just beyond. Ginny was going on about why she was going to give Juan the brush-off, and Bren, half jealous and half enjoying the idea of boys getting punished, was egging her on. A gang of juniors came shrieking around the corner of the building, and Eva's pelt stirred uncomfortably at the sound, the massed voices of humans, the pack-cry. The whole air was full of the same noise, nearer and farther, and every sitting place was filled, like a roost of starlings, as the out-shift gathered to wait for the in-shift to finish with the classrooms so that they could take their turn. It could have been worse. There were schools in the city that operated on a three-shift system, but they were mostly in the poorer areas. On the wall beyond Ginny a couple of older kids were creating their own little bubble of privacy in a long, motionless kiss. Ginny had gotten around to describing Juan's eating habits, and Bren was giggling at each fresh exaggeration. They didn't seem to notice the pressure either. It was as if you were born used to it, the clamor and the jostling, people, people, people. They were the air you breathed, the sea you swam in. But if you weren't people, you stifled, you drowned . . .

This feeling of pressure, of loneliness and strangeness in the crowd, was different from the sort of depression and sadness Eva still sometimes woke with, when she lay remembering how her old body used to enjoy lying in its bed, the caress of nightgown and warm sheets on smooth soft skin. She could take a shot of her dope when those ghost feelings got too strong, though she didn't often need to these days. But this was something else, a mirror image almost, not what the human part of her felt about being chimp but what the chimp felt about being human.

The pressure rose as Ginny and Bren talked across her. Mostly they were very good, they tried hard, but when they got excited they forgot to include her in their glances. Anyway, she wasn't interested in Juan. She shrank into herself and as she did so became aware of a different ghost. It had no body, only a voice, the ghost of a cry, but so strong and near in her mind that every hair on her body stood out. She had heard it just once, weeks ago, when she'd been scampering along the hospital corridor to inspect her new gym, the call of a chimp, scared, lost and bewildered, and waiting—though it couldn't know it—to have its own mind emptied away so that a human mind could invade and explore human pathways through the now blank cells. Where was that chimp now, that mind, those memories? Where was Kelly? Lost . . . lost . . . lost . . .

She was moving before she understood what was happening. The violence of the reaction whirled her off through the gaps between the little knots of kids and then with a leap, clutch, and swing up on to the shoulder of the old robed female statue—Mathematics or History or something—that stood by the library steps. She crouched there in her blue overalls while the cry shuddered up through her. Lost . . . lost . . . lost . . . It echoed off the walls of the Language Building, the lonely cry of a ghost.

For a moment the clamor stopped. A couple of hundred heads turned to stare. Some of the kids laughed and waved arms in greeting as though she were doing something clever. The mood died. She swung down and knuckled back to Bren and Ginny.

"What was that about?" said Bren.

"Did I say something stupid?" said Ginny, the same instant.

Eva made a forget-it grunt. A few minutes later the hooter

sounded, calling the out-shift in to fill their heads with another ration of knowledge.

Eva went home on the school bus. There'd been a fuss about that. The company had wanted to send a car so that Cormac could ride with her—he wasn't allowed on the bus. Eva thought this was ridiculous; though Mom's job was pretty useful and Dad's was quite high up, they only just mustered enough points between them to qualify for a car license, but Eva could have had one from the SMI quota, just for being famous. Only it wouldn't have gotten her through the jams in the car lanes any faster, while the school bus could whisk her home in the bus lanes. How could you kidnap someone out of a bus in the bus lanes—you'd need to hijack another bus to start with . . . Anyway, the company had given in in the end.

After Bren had gotten off the bus Eva sat by herself, staring out over the endless lines of car roofs, and at a jam-packed traveler, and the crowds on the pavement waiting for a gap to board it. People, people . . . They were strange, listless, empty. As if they didn't have anything to live for. Even Ginny and Bren, who seemed so lively, were only lively for today. They never thought about the future or what was going to happen to them when they grew up. Their future was tomorrow or next week or next vacation . . .

Eva gazed at the people, full of a sense of not belonging. She was as different from all of them as if she'd come from another planet, especially so today. Her outburst in the morning had left her both alarmed and exhilarated, which was strange but she thought she knew why. Mom and Dad had taught her to loathe quarrels. You stayed calm, you bottled your anger up, if someone else was in a rage you kept clear of them, and if you did get into a fight you felt sick about it for days—but that was the old Eva. Now there was Kelly too—not the old Kelly either. She was gone, with all her memories, all her sense of belonging and being herself in a particular time and place. She would never come back. But still she had left part of herself behind, her nature, her instincts, still rooted deep into the body into which the human Eva had been grafted. That was the Kelly Eva herself had invited back across the shadowy border between mind and brain. She couldn't do that and then say okay, but I don't want all of her. I'll have the lightning reactions but not the tantrums, the warmth and fun but not the sullen hours, the sympathy but not the mischief. They were Eva too now. She couldn't bottle them away . . . She remembered the relief that had washed through her after that outburst and how she'd settled down at once to grooming Bren's hair. Just like a chimp in the Pool after a fight. Of course.

Cormac met her at the bus stop, and she was glad to see him. He was huge and strong, very neat in his movements, but simpleminded as a child. He thought of her as an animal, somebody's pet, and rumpled her pelt with absentminded fingers and blinked with surprise when she spoke. Sometimes this was irritating, but today it was fine. Cormac knew the difference. She sat in the crook of his arm while they rode the traveler and then knuckled along in his wake for the last stretch. Cormac was big enough for people to stand out of his way, and the crowds, used to the little procession by now, would leave a space for Eva and say "Hi!" to her as she passed, and she'd grin and wave a hand. Most days this was rather good, with its sense of acceptance, of friendliness from strangers, but today the feeling of not belonging was too strong and she kept her eyes on the ground and tried to pretend they weren't there.

Dad had been away two weeks on a lecture tour—a slice of Eva's fame. He was one of those people who can't eat and talk at the same time, so supper took longer than usual while he told Mom how well it had gone. Eva didn't listen much. There was something about Dad in his triumphant moods, though he was a pretty good lecturer—everyone said so . . .

". . . interested to see how the next two experiments turn out," he said and took another mouthful.

In the pause Eva suddenly realized what he'd been talking about.

"Just two, Dad?"

"At the moment. Do you know, Joan's outfit has had more than sixty volunteers, last count?"

"How many chimps?"

"Nothing like enough. If we were to refuse any fresh research projects in other fields, we might have seven candidates by the end of the year."

"Seven volunteers?"

Dad had tried to stop the conversation by taking another mouthful.

"I heard a chimp calling in the hospital," said Eva. "First day I was really up. He didn't sound like a volunteer."

"Caesar," said Dad.

"How's he doing?"

"Too soon to say. Are you going to insist on discussing this, darling?"

"Please."

"All right. As you know, I've never really liked the business of selling chimps for research and have always been very selective about projects. If it had not been for their research value, there would be no chimps in the world today. If we didn't continue to sell the surplus, there would be no Pool."

"Yes, I know, but . . ."

"But what?"

Now Eva wished she hadn't started. Her horror of talking about it like this made it difficult to think.

"This is different. You've saved my life, but you've lost Kelly's. One chimp, one human. It isn't enough."

"You mean that to justify the sacrifice of a chimp, one ought to be able to see the possibility of saving tens of thousands of human lives by the consequent research? I'd have to ask a philosopher if that made the difference. Let me put it another way. Suppose I went out sailing with my daughter and a young chimp, and the boat capsized and I had the chance to save one of you but not both—you wouldn't expect me to save the chimp, would you?"

"I sometimes think so," said Mom, meaning to make a joke of it but getting it wrong.

"Nonsense. It would be no choice at all. That was effectively the same decision we had to make about you. And then if I can make it in your case, what right have I to withhold a similar chance from someone else? Suppose I were in my boat with a chimp and a stranger's child . . ."

"There's millions times more people than there's chimps," said Eva.

It was an argument Eva'd heard him use himself, making the case for more funds for his precious Pool. He remembered and laughed but changed tack.

"All right," he said. "Let's come down to a more selfish level. Do you want to be the only person on whom this procedure has been carried out?"

Dad was deliberately not looking at Mom, but Eva felt her stiffen.

"I don't know," she said.

"You must have thought about it."

She could hear the wariness in his voice and tried to lighten her answer.

"A little. I keep changing my mind. Your idea is we'll go along to the Pool and I'll choose a sexy male and you'll find some boy with an IQ of a hundred and eighty who's just walked under a bus, and then Joan will put them together and we'll have a lovely wedding and live happily ever after?"

Dad laughed. Mom didn't.

"I hadn't gotten that far," said Dad, but Eva had heard in the laugh and the silence that this was something they'd talked about, often.

"Our babies would be just chimps, wouldn't they?" said Eva. "They'd be Kelly's, really."

The tension screw tightened another half turn. They'd talked about this too. Dad chose to answer in his new voice, the shaper scholar, the patient but charming zoologist, explaining to dimwits. Eva felt a prickle of irritation down her spine. He shouldn't use that voice inside the family. It was his way, she guessed, of ducking the dangerous parts of her question (was she going to be allowed to have babies? If so, whose? How? With a real mate or by artificial insemination? And what a frenzy there'd be in the fame market when it happened! The riot outside the apartment the night of that first program would be nothing!).

"That raises a very interesting point," said Dad. "Of course you're right in the sense that such a baby would inherit no human genetic material; but like humans, chimps are not solely the product of their inheritance. They are also creatures of their own cultures, though to a lesser extent than humans. The literature about wild chimps shows that different groups had their different ways of doing things, using simple tools and so on, which the young learned from their elders. Our own chimps would be lost if they had to return to a real jungle, because no one has taught them how to survive under such conditions, but on the other hand they have learned new skills and social arrangements to cope with conditions in the Pool. The social conditions are especially important because the restricted space has imposed a greater need for control of antisocial behavior, and the successful males in particular are those with greater social skills and awareness. It is extremely hard to quantify, but I am beginning to believe that especially in the Reserve, where the natural-selective process has the most chance to operate, something very like an increase in intelligence is becoming perceptible . . .''

"But what about *my* babies?" said Eva.

"I was coming to that. The young of all higher animals are learning-machines. Evolution has programmed them to learn. The bigger brains they have, the more knowledge they can file and store. In all experiments with chimp learning the teachers have been humans, apart from a few anecdotal instances where a human-taught chimp has passed on some detail to another chimp. Moreover, the material taught has been strongly human biased—language is the obvious example. But imagine a chimp mother with human intelligence living in the wild. What would *she* teach her babies? Survival skills that they do not already possess—how to make fire, perhaps . . .''

"Knots?"

"Knots is an excellent example. Knots require dexterity and intelligence, both at about the limit of natural chimp capacity. The brighter ones could tie knots, the less bright couldn't. Now suppose the ability to tie knots conferred an advantage in evolutionary terms, and suppose the knowledge of how to do it was passed on through a number of generations, then you would find that you had been breeding for dexterity and intelligence. You would have bred something into the chimp gene. A gift from humankind."

Dad was really excited now, not just acting. His eyes sparkled, and his beard wagged. If he'd had a mane of white hair, he'd have been tossing it around. You couldn't help liking him in this mood, though Mom, Eva was aware, had switched right off and withdrawn into herself as though all she could bear to think about was the process of cutting her food up on her plate and then chewing and swallowing it, with no enjoyment at all. Now, still chewing, she got up and began to clear the main course away. Eva scurried to help her.

"Don't bother," said Mom. "Go on talking to Dad."

She was much more upset than Eva had realized. It was going to be difficult to get Dad to switch tracks in this mood. Eva went back to the table, peeled a banana, and ate it slowly, enjoying every mouthful but waiting for a gap in the flow.

"Now, suppose you introduce into your group a mutation," said Dad. "Not anything physical, just some quirk, some trait, something like a slightly greater ability to intuit the causes of things, the why as well as the how . . ."

In the pause for breath Eva made her grunt and rattled out her question.

"Are they getting bananas at the Pool?"

"Bananas all around? Can't afford it. Where was I?"

"Hey! What about all these extra funds I'm earning for the benefit of the Pool?"

"They're for research and so on. I was saying . . ."

"Bananas are benefits if you're a chimp."

"Okay, when we're really rolling. But to go back . . ."

"You better take me up on Saturday. I'll do an opinion poll, find out how they want you to spend their funds. Okay?"

You could use the box like that, pressing the keys while the other person was still talking. Somehow it forced even Dad to wait and see what you were going to say. He shrugged and gave up.

"I want to be with the others anyway," said Eva.

"No," said Mom.

She was standing in the doorway from the kitchen, looking as though someone had just died.

"No, darling," she said again. "I won't have it."

Eva's hand froze over the keys.

"Now, listen, darling," said Dad. "What we think, Mom and I is this . . ."

Eva didn't listen—she just understood. Mom didn't want her to go to the Pool. She couldn't bear the idea of Eva living that kind of life. Not at all, not even for a few hours at a time. She'd argued with Dad about it. Dad disagreed—he'd known it was something that Eva was going to need, and besides, it might have been extremely useful with his work, because Eva would learn about chimp behavior almost like a spy. She'd find out things no one had known before. He probably still wanted that, but he wasn't prepared to fight for it, so he'd let Mom have her way for the time being, hoping that in a year or two Mom wouldn't mind so much; and in the meanwhile the whole business they'd just been talking about, giving her others like her, chimps with human minds . . . well they were going to do it anyway, but it was a sort of compromise, Dad's way of putting things, to keep everyone sort-of-happy . . .

Eva picked up her mug and slung it at the wall. It smashed. By then she was on the table, flailing the dishes onto the door with a sweep of her arm. Mom screamed. Dad yelled at Eva to stop it. She ignored him and sprang across the room to the window, grabbed at the slats of the blind and ripped it down. Mom was shouting "No! Eva! No!" Dad was at his desk with his back to the room. He turned. He had a stun gun in his hand, the sort they used at the Pool to knock out a chimp they couldn't handle any other way. As he raised it Eva snatched up a cushion and flung it at the gun, spoiling his aim. Before he could steady his arm she was on him. He tried to hang on, but she was far too strong. She wrenched the gun from his fingers and backed off. Mom was crying. Eva faced Dad, panting.

Her whole body was still electric with the impulse to rush around the apartment, breaking and destroying. She had watched the eruption almost as if from the outside, powerless to stop it, only able to direct it a little, using her human intelligence to recognize the gun, throw the cushion, snatch the weapon away. Now, with a big effort, she forced herself to stand still and tap out a sentence. Deliberately she didn't press any of the tone codes.

"If you won't let me be a chimp there, then I'll be a chimp here," said the lifeless voice. Dad watched her, fright and fury in the set of his mouth, calculation in his eyes. He'd kept the gun ready and loaded, Eva thought. He'd known, really. She pointed it downward and pressed the trigger. Phut, thud. The fine-needled dart quivered in the carpet. Mom stared at it, gulping to control her sobs. Eva pressed the keys again, but this time she coded in the human warmth.

"I'm sorry. It's there. It's part of me now. Please understand."

Silence still.

"It doesn't mean I'll stop loving you."

Dad turned and fiddled with the ruined blind, pretending he was trying to see whether it could be mended. Eva put the gun on the desk and went and stood in front of Mom in the half-crouched position now natural to her, with one set of knuckles on the ground. She looked up into Mom's face. The blue eyes were blank, not stony and rejecting but empty, numb, lightless. Eva's whole instinct was to reach up and touch and caress, but she knew that would be a mistake. Mom managed an unhappy smile.

"I suppose I'll have to say yes," she said.

She turned and went back into the kitchen.

MONTH SIX, DAY TEN

A new life, a beginning . . .
Sun on a naked pelt . . .
Chimp odors, chimp voices . . .

Shivering with nerves, Eva waited. The rusty surface of a branch pressed its hard nodules into her soles. The iron trunk at her side was rougher and rustier still. In front of her rose a whole grove of iron trees, gaunt, leafless, five regular lines of them stretching away into the distance, rising from a barren gray floor whose pits and boulders had the same square, unnatural angles as the trees. Around the grove was a low cliff, with openings like the mouths of caves, only here again the square angles and straight edges showed that, like everything else she could see, the caves had been made by people.

Eva hadn't guessed she would find it so weird. She had seen it before, often, but with human eyes. Then the trees had been the iron pillars that had once supported the roof of a large factory; the boulders had been beds for heavy machinery; the surrounding caves had been offices and storerooms. Beyond the roofless walls she could see the tops of the rest of the human forest, building beyond building, rising into the morning sky. The only reason that there were no high rises here was that the ground below was riddled with the tunnels of an exhausted coal mine, so in the old days the area had been used for industry. But then, Dad said, the tides of money had washed elsewhere and the area had become derelict, just at the time when the last chimpanzees were being gathered out of the wild to form the Pool. Of course, most of the people who'd done the agitating and signed the petitions had thought the chimps could come and live in a nice green park some-where, like squirrels, but being chimps they'd have stripped the precious trees leafless in a couple of months. Instead, they'd been put in this iron-and-concrete grove. It used to seem neat and convenient when Dad explained it, but it didn't now, not through chimp eyes. It seemed weird.

These ruined factories were the Reserve Section of the Pool. From here came the chimps in Dad's Research Section, and the ones who were sold to other scientists, and slightly luckier ones for people to go and look at it in the cities. But this was their jungle now, where as far as possible they were left alone. Ropes had been hung from some of the girders, like creepers in a real jungle, and extra branches had been bolted to the pillars to make them easier to climb. Eva was squatting on one now. She couldn't see the whole area even of this particular factory, because low walls had been built here and there across the floor space to make a kind of open maze, carefully sited so that the chimps could have corners to explore and feel private while human observers could still study most of what was going on from observation points up in the outer walls.

Dad was in one of these now, with Joey, the head keeper at the Reserve. They had a long-range stun gun loaded and ready —Mom had insisted on that, and had made Eva promise she wouldn't go anywhere out of Joey's line of sight—but neither Eva nor Dad thought there'd be that sort of trouble. Chimp groups weren't like beehives or ants' nests, so close-knit that they'd kill a stranger who tried to join them. In the old jungle, Dad said, females had mostly stuck together in loose family networks—daughters, aunts, cousins—while the males had wandered around more. And nowadays the Pool was always swapping individuals from one section to another without any fuss, though sometimes it took them a day or two to fit in, and there were always a few who, like humans, were just plain unpopular. There was no reason why Eva shouldn't be okay, but still she was extremely nervous. She felt as though the next hour might be the most important in her whole new life.

She sniffed at the chimpy air and listened to the voices echoing among the iron trees—squabbles, happy noises, the chitter-chatter of a baby pretending to be in trouble. The urge rose in her throat to answer, to cry her lonely call, to make them come and find her. She controlled it. That wasn't how she wanted to start.

She'd been sitting in her tree for something like twenty minutes when a young adult male came rambling down past one of the machine beds and saw her. She didn't know his name—she'd only known the chimps in the Research Section that well. She gave him the breathy hoot of greeting, but he had something else on his mind and knuckled on out of sight. Still, the encounter calmed her nerves slightly—at least he'd seemed to think it was perfectly normal for this stranger to be sitting up there.

Another time passed by—she didn't know how long, she'd stopped thinking in minutes. Then a group of chimps emerged from one of the roofless rooms on the far side and came wandering toward where Eva sat. Three adult females and a four-year-old—Beth, Dinks, Lana, Buttons; Beth's son, Abel, one-and-a-half; Lana's baby, Wang. (The Pool staff took turns to name the chimps.) This was the group Eva had been waiting for. They usually made their way over here this time of the morning. She knew their names because Dad had shown her shapings of them last night.

Beth was elderly, gray around the ears, with a long, thin face; Dinks was an orphan who'd been sort of adopted by Beth a few years back when her own daughter had been sold for research; Buttons had been miserable in one of the public areas, so had been brought here and had just joined herself on to

Beth's group; Lana was Beth's niece. She was also Kelly's sister. Their mother, Arlene, had died last winter, while Kelly had lain inert in the long dream, having her mind emptied away and then slowly being turned into Eva. This was the group Kelly would naturally have belonged to if she'd never been taken off for research. It seemed the obvious one to try. Only, without actually saying anything to each other, Dad and Eva had agreed they wouldn't tell Mom.

Either they didn't notice Eva sitting halfway up a tree in "their" patch, or they just ignored her. They came closer and closer. Her heart pounded. Her lips began to ripple with exploratory impulses of greeting and beseeching. And then, frustratingly, they settled out of sight on the far side of a piece of wall that ran slantwise across the floor a few paces from Eva's perch. Perhaps, she realized, they *had* noticed her and didn't want to be watched by this stranger. She sat for a while, listening to the faint sounds they made. On the whole, unless they were having a squabble or one of them was frustrated in some way, chimps didn't "talk" with their voices. Most of that sort of noise was used for calls—"Danger!" "Hurry!" "Food!" Their language when they were resting peaceably was grimace and gesture and touch. Touch especially. All Eva could tell without seeing them was that one of them—probably Abel— was restless and being a nuisance, pestering the others to play. Nothing else happened, not here, though over on the far side of the space a real hullabaloo blew up between two males and then died away.

After a while Eva climbed down from her tree, knuckled back toward the outer wall, and picked up a plastic soda bottle she'd noticed lying there. The staff deliberately dropped bits of harmless junk into the space to give the chimps objects to play with and use. On her way back she found a strip of coarse woven stuff. She hunkered down in the open just beyond the wall, about a dozen paces from Beth's group and began to unpick the cloth. The strands came out about half a meter long. Slowly she tied them together. The knots were surprisingly difficult, not just because the chimp thumb is so short and awkward but because her fingers didn't seem to understand what was expected of them. It was like tying knots in a dream. She managed to tie four strands into a length and then looped one end around the neck of the bottle and pulled it tight.

All this while she pretended to be absorbed in what she was doing, but she was aware that by now most of Beth's group had stopped reacting with one another and were watching her. Her spine prickled with their attention. Close in front of her there was a gap in the floor level, some kind of sump or inspection pit; it was dry, so it must drain away somewhere, but it had a jumble of rubbish in the bottom, old cabbage stalks and peelings, pieces of plastic, cans, cardboard. She dropped the bottle over the edge and backed away, holding the cord.

Her move took her beyond the edge of the wall, out of sight of the others. Hunkering down again she pulled on the cord, teasing the bottle up over the edge of the pit and then, slowly, across the floor toward her.

There was a scamper of feet—Abel, probably—and a bark— Beth calling him back. Eva whisked the bottle out of sight and hid it behind her back. Abel came rushing to the corner and stared, bewildered. Eva laughed at him. She went back to the pit, still holding the bottle so that he couldn't see it, and dropped it over the edge again, then backed off, but this time not so far, so that the others could see what she was doing. When she pulled the cord Abel followed the bottle across the floor, crouching so close that his face almost touched it, but as soon as he made a move to grab it Eva whisked it out of reach. She hid it and laughed again, then turned. Lana, she saw, was laughing too. A chimp's laugh is almost silent, a sucking of breath and a round toothless grin. Abel, suddenly alarmed, went scuttering back to Beth. Beth rose slowly from where Dinks had been grooming her and came over. Her solid, deliberate movement showed she was boss of the group and knew it and expected this stranger to know it too. Eva crouched low and gave a series of brief, quiet pants—what Dad called "submission greeting," a way of saying You're the boss. Beth snorted, then lowered her head to within a few inches of Eva's and stared.

Eva couldn't stare back because that would have been a challenge; but flickering glances showed her there was something else in Beth's eyes than the assertion of dominance—puzzlement? Surprise? Eva was very aware now of her differences, of the people smells she must carry, shampoo and cooking and trafficky streets, and inside her the human mind trying to control the encounter. She made more submission pants and put out her left hand in a tentative pleading gesture. Beth backed away, still staring, but now with a frown of definite bewilderment. Almost as clear as speaking her look said Where have I seen you before?

Chimps had good memories, Eva knew. When she was five a young female called Snoo had been very fond of her and wanted to play with her all the time whenever Eva came. But then Snoo had gone off for a language experiment and Eva hadn't seen her for three whole years, so that Eva had changed a lot before they met again. Even so, Snoo had known her at once and gone wild with excitement, jumping up and down and shrieking in her glee. So was it possible Beth actually remembered Kelly? Dad had said no. Chimps for the Research Section were taken away when they were still small, in order not to disrupt the community too much, so Kelly would have been less than a year old—tiny, when Beth had last seen her. It didn't seem possible. Still . . .

She tried the greeting again, but this time more confidently —not Good morning, Lady Elizabeth but Hi, Mrs. Beth. Beth gave up the puzzle, whooshed her breath out, and lumbered back to Dinks. Eva stayed where she was and made a loose loop in the end of her cord.

After a short while Abel came sliding across to look for the bottle. Eva rolled it toward him, then drew it back, coaxing him along till he was in reach. She picked the bottle up and teased him closer, then slipped the loop over his neck as she gave him the bottle. He grabbed and scampered away to play with his toy, not yet realizing it was fastened to him. After a while he took it to the pit and dropped it over the edge. Nothing happened, so he lost interest and moved off. As soon as the cord tightened he jerked away. The bottle shot into the open. Abel stared at it, nosed forward, and then backed off again. The bottle followed him. Now for the first time he seemed to notice the cord. He grabbed it and pulled, jerking the bottle nearer. Suddenly he seemed to lose his alarm and started running to and fro, trailing the bottle behind him, delighted by its rattle across the concrete, dropping it into the pit and yanking it out again, until the weak cord snapped. For a minute or two he simply ran about, trailing the cord, but there was no fun in that, so he lost his temper and wrenched the cord off his neck.

The adults had watched his game intently, their heads moving to and fro as he scampered about. When it was over Beth and Dinks went back to grooming but Lana turned toward Eva with a look of amusement crinkling around her eyes. They laughed together. Eva rose and lolloped across, then stopped. There was still, she sensed, an invisible barrier that it wasn't polite to go bursting through. Slowly she reached out with the same pleading gesture she had used toward Beth, but stretching farther, farther. Lana replied by pushing an arm toward her. Eva touched with her fingertips, walking them delicately up the flesh beneath the dark hairs, and then, when Lana didn't withdraw, hunkered down closer and began to groom her never-known sister in earnest.

It was some while before she realized that she had broken her promise by moving out of Joey's line of fire. By then she was sitting huddled close to Lana while Lana searched steadily down her shoulder blade and Wang scrambled his way over the pair of them, not seeming to notice which was which. Eva hadn't had a bath for four days, but she knew she must still smell strongly of the human world. Lana sniffed at her sometimes, inquisitively but not suspiciously. Sitting in the sun, being properly groomed by a real chimp who did it because she wanted to and not just because she was supposed to was the most glorious sensation. Eva had never felt closer to anyone. The only trouble was that Lana wasn't going to find any reward for her search. She didn't seem to mind, but Eva had picked off and nibbled half a dozen little bugs that had moved in under Lana's fur.

I must get me some bugs of my own, she thought. Mom's not going to like that.

"How was it, darling?"

"Okay. A little like the first day of school. I think some of them sort of guessed I was funny, but then they forgot."

Mom had tried to make her question casual but you could hear the edge in it. Eva, on the other hand, could control her tone exactly, using the box. It wasn't fair, but it couldn't be helped.

"I'm going to find lots out for Dad," she said.

"Good."

Not fair, either. Eva was preparing Mom to accept that she was going back to the Pool as often as she could. At the same time she was concealing the argument she'd had with Dad, first because of moving out of sight and then by losing all track of time, so that in order to attract her attention he'd had to break the Reserve rule of not making the chimps aware of the human presence more than he had to. Still, she was fairly certain he wouldn't tell Mom. He was too excited about the new project of having Eva see if she could teach any of Beth's group to tie knots, and then whether they would pass the skill on.

Eva felt odd about all this. She had always been so open with Mom in the old days, so close and trusting. Now, though she was a little ashamed and guilty about what was happening, it was only a little. It was like the pang you get looking through old photographs and seeing someone who used to be a best friend but you haven't thought about for years. I *must* write her a card, you tell yourself, and perhaps you do, but that's all.

Eva pressed the keys again, coding in pleasure and excitement.

"I made a friend," she said.

"That's nice," said Mom automatically, but stopped her next sentence before she'd begun it. Why don't you ask her over? it would have been, but that didn't make sense now.

MONTH SIX,
DAY ELEVEN

Living two lives . . .
Yesterday the Reserve, the silent iron trees, the
sunlight . . .
Friendly fingers creeping across a shoulder blade . . .
Peace . . .
Today clamor, scurry, pressure . . .
Today people . . .

Bobo snatched off Jenny's glasses and bit them in two. One of Mr. Coulis's helpers tried to grab him, but he flung her away, snarling. Mr. Coulis himself came hurrying but stopped when Bobo lurched at him with his hair bushed out under his cowboy shirt—a male chimp's bite is a serious wound. Realizing his advantage but already scared of what he'd done, Bobo looked for an escape. Up, his instincts told him. He leaped for a nearby lighting tower. The technician at the top felt the tower shake and shouted, then looked over and saw Bobo swarming up. He scuttered down the ladder on the far side. Bobo reached the platform and turned, barking his anger. When he shook the guardrail the whole tower rattled and quivered and two loose lights fell off, their bulbs exploding when they hit the ground. The noise excited him further. Everyone was yelling now. Mr. Coulis had started to climb the ladder, but Bobo saw him coming and slung a screwdriver at him, hitting him on the cheek. He scrambled down with blood beginning to stream onto his shirt. Bobo tried to wrench a fixed light off the rail.

Mimi began to screech. She was a shaper director, quite well known for her pictures and even better known for her extravagance and tantrums. She was a short, square, yellow-faced woman who always wore red-and-black outfits with chunky necklaces and bangles. In a tantrum she threw her arms about so that the bangles clashed out of key with her screeches. Mr. Coulis tried to placate her with little bobs and shrugs while he dabbed at his cheek with a bloody handkerchief. It wasn't his fault. The script had called for a *big* chimp, and that meant a male. Bobo hadn't done commercials before, but he'd always been fairly easygoing and less unpredictable than the other males. And so on. Mimi paid no attention.

The four trained chimps—Jenny, Belinda, Olo, Nin—watched both exhibitions with wariness. They probably found the human quarrel more frightening. To see a male chimp in a rage was an everyday thing for them, but to see humans making the same kind of noises, giving the same kind of signals, especially to Mr. Coulis, whom they'd been trained to regard as dominant—that was new and alarming. Humans had immense and magical powers. What mightn't one of *them* do in a tantrum?

Eva also watched, but with increasing exasperation. She hated these sessions anyway, but it was in the contract so she had to do them. In a minute or two Mr. Coulis would have to lay Bobo out with his stun gun, and that would mean no more filming today and trying again tomorrow. Tomorrow she wanted to go back to the Reserve. After that it would be at least two weeks before she got another chance to spend time with Lana, to sit in the sun and groom and be groomed and watch Wang learning the rules of the concrete grove. Eva's diary was full for three days after that, and then for the next ten she'd be in estrus. This happened once every thirty-five days—your sex parts on your rump swelled up and became tender and the males got excited about you. There were pills

Eva could have used to suppress it, but they made her feel sick and low. Being in estrus didn't bother Eva herself much—far less than she'd expected—and the males at the Reserve wouldn't have done anything unless she'd let them, but they'd have hung around and begged, and she'd have felt she was making a difference between herself and the other females by shooing them off—and anyway, Mom wouldn't have dreamed of letting her go to the Reserve like that. By the time estrus was over it would be school again.

Of course she understood why Bobo was upset. Partly it was the lights and Mimi's beads and the scurry of humans trying to get things done under pressure, but mainly it was something else. Bobo was a young adult male. In his Public Section there were three males older and stronger than him, but here he might have been boss over the five females, given the chance. But there was Mr. Coulis here, and all these other humans, and besides he'd lived most of his life in Research, and now in a Public Area, both of which were even less natural than the Reserve. He didn't know where to begin. His solution was the usual male one—he threw a tantrum.

"I'm on the big fellow's side, myself," said a man's voice close by.

"I don't care. I want my coffee break," said a woman.

Eva sat by herself between takes, not just because there was a chair marked EVA but because anything else was impossible. She was too conscious of her difference from the other chimps to stay with them—in this world they were chimps but she was people—but she didn't feel like talking to people either. Her only thought was to get the whole thing over with and go away. Now she merely glanced sideways and saw the couple, a pretty woman with a bored face and a plump young man with a pale gold beard. He noticed Eva's glance and smiled.

"How about you, miss?" he said.

Eva grunted, a no-meaning sound.

"It's just against reason and nature," said the man, still speaking to Eva. "Bringing a noble beast like that into this kind of crappy setup and getting him to do anything we fancy, such as being dressed up for laughs in a cowboy outfit. It makes me sick."

"It's a living," said the woman.

"God, now look! They're going to knock him out!" said the man.

Mr. Coulis was checking the stun gun over. Exasperation flooded through Eva. In a couple of seconds she'd have been up among the lights, screeching and throwing like Bobo, but she just managed to control her fury. She picked up her keyboard from the floor beside her and tapped out a sentence.

"Tell them to turn the lights off."

The young man nodded and turned away. Eva handed the keyboard to the woman and knuckled across the floor to where Mr. Coulis was raising the stun gun to take aim. He didn't see her coming until she reached up and pulled the muzzle down. He looked at her, astonished. She shook her head like a human and held up her free hand, palm forward, in a signal for him to wait.

Bobo, sensing that he was losing his audience's attention, began jumping up and down, making his tower clatter to his rhythm.

Then the main lights went out. Though there were still a few ordinary houselights burning, the effect was like sudden dusk, a forest dark, especially up above among the looped and trailing cables. Bobo was startled into silence. Everyone waited.

Eva knuckled across to the group of females and faced them. They were all, of course, young, used to being bossed by adults and also by humans. They were frightened too, grinning and showing their teeth. Belinda was the brightest of them. Eva held out her hand to her, palm up, moving her forearm gently to and fro, the standard Please help gesture. With four flat fingers she pointed to the tower. Please help again. Then she took Belinda by the wrist and gave a little tug. The other three watched, frightened still but with their grins less toothy. They all understood what Eva wanted. They must all have seen the adult females in the Public Section ganging up, three or four together, to counteract the bullying of one of the males.

Eva turned, still holding Belinda's wrist but using her free arm to knuckle across to the tower. Belinda didn't resist. At the foot of the tower Eva let go and began to climb. When she reached the first strut she stopped and looked down. Belinda was hesitating, one hand on an upright, but the other three were now moving, half hypnotized, to join her. Eva beckoned encouragingly and climbed on. Above her, Bobo had stopped his jumping and had begun to screech. The whole studio rang with the racket, but Eva knew it wasn't as terrifying as it sounded to human ears. To the chimps it meant something different—Bobo himself was scared. Strong as he was he couldn't cope with five females if they chose to attack him.

She swung herself across to the far side of the tower and swarmed rapidly up, coming out on the platform behind Bobo, who was still watching her allies climbing the side of the tower that faced out into the studio. She knuckled across, reached up and touched him on the shoulder. He jumped several inches and spun around, his face one enormous grin with his big emergent canines gleaming in the gloom.

Eva, the moment she'd touched him, had backed off, crouched down, and begun the quick pants of submission. Bobo stared, baffled. He didn't notice the heads of the allies appearing over the rim of the platform. They too stared for a moment, then hesitatingly swung themselves on to the platform and gave Bobo the same signal Eva was giving. Olo pre-

sented him her rump, but since she was wearing jeans this
didn't have any effect.

Bobo sat down. His grin was still huge, but his teeth were
hardly showing at all now. Eva immediately crouched beside
him and started grooming attentively through the fur of his
neck. Nin joined on the other side, and the remaining three
settled into a huddle to groom one another. The humans muttered below, a gentle, almost pleasing sound. Then the whole
group tensed as someone started to climb the ladder. Bobo
stirred apprehensively, though Eva did her best to calm him
with comforting little clicks. As soon as Mr. Coulis's face appeared above the edge of the platform she held up her hand
toward him, fingers spread. Five minutes. The face ducked out
of sight.

Jenny and Olo swung themselves across and peered over to
watch Mr. Coulis going down the ladder. When they came
back they looked at Eva for several seconds, and then Olo
settled beside her and began to search through her nape hairs.
Bobo turned, put his arm around her, and gave her the big,
open-mouthed chimp kiss. He did it without thinking, of
course. It was what he wanted to do. He'd always been a naturally gentle and affectionate chimp.

By the time the five minutes were up they were a group,
understanding one another and fitting comfortably together.
Bobo was the official boss and got the little signs of respect
and submission, but he knew and so did the others that the
sensible thing was to follow Eva's lead. She was the one who'd
settled things, calmed Bobo down by giving him what he
wanted but didn't know how to get, calmed the humans down
too, and stopped their screeching, made the mad world sensible for a moment, and known the signal to send the dominant
human back down the ladder. When eventually she rose and
beckoned to them to follow, they all climbed down without a
fuss. Somebody had had the sense to produce a bunch of

bananas. Eva tore it in two, gave half to Bobo and shared the rest among her allies.

As soon as the first take was over—of course it didn't go smoothly because nothing with chimps and nothing with shaper people ever did—Mr. Coulis took his chimps off out of sight to a large cage where they could be alone. Eva went back to her chair at the edge of the studio. The woman had gone, but the young man with the beard was waiting with her keyboard.

"That worked out pretty damn well," he said. "First time in years I've seen my mother upstaged."

"Uh?"

"Yeah. I don't belong. I'm Mimi Venturi's son. We got into an argument about whether she should have taken this assignment on. You know how it happened? Honeybear was all set to stop using chimps in their ads and go in for swanky-arty, so they hired my mother. Then you showed up, and they decided to stick with the chimps. They wanted to back out of their contract, but my mother needed the money, so they said okay, but in that case you've got to direct the chimps. My mother says chimps are hell, but they're less hell than actors, and, anyway, who am I to tell her she's wasting her talents. I say the hell with your talents, you're wasting chimps. She says they love it. I say crap. She says come and see. Now I've seen."

"They like it when people gave them fruit. Otherwise, no."

"I'll tell her."

"I hate it all, but the Pool needs the money."

"Same the whole world over."

"At least I can go home after. What's your name?"

"Call me Grog. It's short for Giorgio. Grog Kennedy, because my mother was married to a guy of that name when I got born. She's had eight husbands, but I wasn't any of theirs.

I guess if you looked in the history books, you could find there've been worse mothers, but I haven't met any."

He sounded perfectly cheerful about it. In fact, it didn't sound as if he minded anything much. You'd have taken him for a very relaxed, easygoing, pleasant young man, if it hadn't been for the vehemence, the passion, that Eva had heard in his voice when she'd been talking to the woman about Bobo's outburst. Eva liked him in a way she didn't often experience nowadays with new people. There was nothing in anything he said, in tone or glance or gesture, that suggested that he didn't find it perfectly normal to be talking to her. Even Bren (even Mom, still) couldn't do that, quite.

"What do you think ought to happen to us?" she said.

"You chimps? You count yourself in?"

"Yes."

"Go back to the jungle. There's about enough left."

"We couldn't live in the jungle, not anymore."

"You're going to have to learn to live somewhere without help from us humans, and soon. We're giving up."

"Uh?"

"Sure. Haven't you noticed? We're opting out, not trying anymore, living in the past. We conquered the planet, and what has it done for us? Zilch. All we've got is one ruined planet. How long d'you think we're going to go on looking after a bunch of monkeys? I tell you, Eva, you better be thinking, and thinking now, how you chimps are going to start getting a living for yourselves without us."

He actually meant it. Eva could hear. Though his voice stayed light and level the passion was back. Eva hadn't meant to talk at all, and even now didn't feel like getting into a serious conversation. She could have explained about the several attempts there'd been in the old days to teach chimps from zoos and research establishments how to live wild and look after themselves, and how difficult it had been, though a

few of them had managed it; but tapping out all that stuff
would have taken so long, and, besides, she wasn't sure of the
details. Grog sounded like the kind of nut case who needed
chapter and verse before he would accept anything.

"You better come over and talk to Dad," she said. "He's
read all the books."

"Like to meet him. Sure that's okay?"

Eva grunted and told him the number to call. He wrote it
down, then squatted cross-legged on the floor beside her. He
seemed to understand her mood and dropped back into his
amused, detached voice, telling her all about himself in a way
that meant she could keep the talk going with just a grunt
here and there. He was twenty-seven, older than he looked.
He didn't have a job because, he said, Mimi bust up anything
he started on; she liked to have him around, he said, as a way
of getting her revenge on men. Marrying them was another
way. In spite of what he said Eva guessed he was actually
rather fond of his mother, but having to cope with her meant
that he didn't have any spare emotions to spend on other
people. Instead, his love, his passion, came out in his feeling
for animals. He wasn't too realistic about it because he hadn't
had much chance to learn what animals are actually like, but
judging by the way he dealt with her, Eva felt he'd pick up
anything he needed very quickly. Without thinking what she
was doing, she started to groom her way up through the short
gold hairs at the corner of his jaw. He accepted her touch
without comment, simply adjusting his position so that she
could work more easily.

The chimps came back for the next take in a jumpy mood,
but as soon as Eva knuckled down to meet them they crowded
around her, panting and touching. Even Bobo half forgot his
dignity and tried to greet her as though she'd been boss. They
needed the reassurance of her presence, the understanding
that nothing unpredictable or ugly would happen to them

while she was around. Very much to her surprise, Eva found that she actually enjoyed the sense of power and respect she got from them. She'd never been a leader in the old days, always more of a tagger-along and seer-what-happened. Now, though, she had to lead. Jenny was a natural tease, with a knack of spoiling any setup just as it was all ready to go. When she noticed this was about to happen Eva would prod Bobo and point, and Bobo would bush his fur out and snarl at Jenny, who would immediately cower and behave. Bobo himself as the day went on became more and more fretful, but the others understood the importance of keeping him happy. Belinda half-accidentally organized a sort of rotation so that Bobo always had a couple of females paying attention to him. By the end of the day Belinda was also trying to copy some of the grunts and gestures that she'd seen Eva using to control the threatening swarm of humans.

The whole thing ended with the shoot-out. It was mostly done by tricks and cameras. Bobo had a gun taped to his hand, and of course he just waved it about and tried to shake it free and pull it off, but by piecing tiny pieces of that together they were going to make it look as if he'd drawn it from his holster. Eva's gun was a trick banana. She drew it and pulled the trigger; the skin split open and the banana shot across the saloon, finishing in Bobo's mouth (more tricks). It all ended with his sitting down and munching away, which he happened actually to do the first time, with exactly the right look of having decided he was tired of being a baddy and was now going to become a model citizen. Pure accident, of course, but all the humans laughed and cheered, as much with the relief of having gotten the assignment over as with real amusement. The studio echoed with their baying cackle. Coming from a Public Area with humans gawking at them all day long, Mr. Coulis's chimps were used to the noise and paid no attention, but Eva felt her whole skin prickle with fright and rage. The urge to

get away was overpowering. She saw a couple of studio assistants coming her way, their kids' autograph books open and
ready. Normally she'd have done what they wanted, but today she swung away and scampered across to where she'd left
her keyboard by her chair. Grog was still standing there, staring at the scene with a look of real hatred.

"Don't forget," she said. "Call Dad."

"Will do."

She grunted and knuckled away to her dressing room.

MONTH EIGHT,
DAYS FOUR AND SIX

Living—just living.
What for?
The apes in the iron grove, waiting, purposeless . . .
The people cramming the pavements, cramming the
travelers, their faces all fret, purposeless . . .
Eva, between . . .
What for?

Grog hit it off fabulously with Mom—with Dad, too, in a
different way. He even managed it with both together. When
he had Dad to himself he let Dad do all the talking, just
asking the odd question to nudge the conversation on. At the
same time, Eva noticed, he gave Dad little signals of deference
while still managing to seem quite free and independent.
With Mom he talked gossip, mostly. Tagging along with Mimi
he'd met shaper stars, artists, billionaires, and they fell naturally into the talk. He had a story about them or knew what
they were really like, and told her. If Dad had been listening
he'd have felt a need to compete with famous people *he'd*
met, and then get huffy because they weren't as famous as
Grog's. And Grog listened. He remembered what Mom told
him—the names and doings of people she tried to help in her
job, and he laughed or sympathized with their stories, and so
on. It seemed perfectly genuine. Eva decided he was just interested in people, in his rather detached way, because they were
people, not because they were famous. She said so one day
and he shook his head.

"Sure, I'm interested," he said. "What you mean is I'm not impressed—just like I'm not impressed by money. I'm interested though, because money's useful. How's old Beth doing?"

Eva gave him the chimp gossip—he was interested in that too. Only later did she wonder whether he'd brought Beth up so as to stop her from asking what he was going to use his famous friends for—he didn't need anything or seem to want anything. She began to watch him with different eyes, noticing, for instance, how when he had Mom and Dad together he would usually side with Mom in an argument, somehow without actually contradicting Dad, and how in these arguments, if they had anything to do with chimps or conservation, Grog seemed better informed each time he came. He must have been reading a lot and watching tapes, but he never said so.

Cormac had a toothache. He was pretending he didn't but Mom, typically, got him to admit it and then insisted on driving him off to find a dentist while Eva was in the Reserve, though the chances of getting emergency treatment in less than six hours were roughly nil. They weren't back by the time Eva came out, so she hid on a wide shelf above some garbage cans that were housed in a shed by the parking lot. The bricks had gaps between them so that the air stayed fresh around the cans, which allowed Eva to watch the entrance for Mom's car. Eva had never really believed that anyone would want to kidnap her, but Dad did, and Honeybear had put it into the contract that she had to have a bodyguard, so there was a good chance Cormac would have been fired if she'd been spotted hanging around alone.

At first she just crouched there, enjoying her peace and privacy, easing herself into the transition between her two lives. Time went by and she began to feel anxious. She could feel her lips tensing and drawing back to show her teeth. Then she heard a familiar voice. "Saturday again, okay?" "Far as I know, Grog." "Right, so long." He strolled past only a few paces away. She was off the shelf and scampering after him before she had time to wonder why he was there. He turned at the sound of her feet and smiled.

"Hi, Eva. Thought you'd gone home."

"Mom's taken Cormac to the dentist. She's late."

"Uh-huh. Had a good time?"

He hadn't seemed even faintly surprised or put out to see her, but now there was something in his tone, in the quickness of the question, trying to put the talk on to ground of his own choosing, which stopped her from answering normally. She grunted an okay and changed the subject.

"Why are you here?"

"Just interested."

"Does Dad know?"

People had to get special permission, with good reasons, to come to the Reserve. The Public Section was for the gawkers.

"Guess not. Didn't want to bother him."

Her grunt this time was surprise and doubt, but at that moment Mom drove into the parking lot.

"No time now," he said. "Don't worry—it's all in a good cause. Tell you about it—uh, when's the next commercial?"

"Day after tomorrow."

"Okay, I'll drive you to the studios. Pick you up half past eight. Tell you on the way. Hi, Lil, good to see you."

"What on earth are you doing up here?"

"Making a date with your daughter."

As usual, he managed it perfectly—teasing, a bit mysterious, making her understand she'd just get teased again if she went on, so that she'd better shut up.

"Tuesday, then," he said. "Eight-fifteen, sharp. Hi, Cormac. See you, Lil."

He strolled away.

"What was that about?" said Mom.

"Don't know—only he's taking me to the studio so he can explain why he's been nosing around. How's your tooth, Cormac?"

Grog's car was characteristic—small and old and smelly. Even more characteristic was the fact that he had a license for it, when he didn't even have a job and didn't do anything for anyone. He kept overriding the City Guidance System to drive manually along side routes that avoided the jams. He didn't seem to want to talk, so Eva decided to ask him directly.

"What were you doing up at the Reserve?"

"Watching. Learning."

"Why?"

"Tell you when we get there. There'll be time."

As he spoke his head moved fractionally. To Cormac, crouching enormous on the backseat, it probably looked just like the result of a jolt, but Eva understood. They reached their destination with a good half hour to spare.

Honeybear rented a studio from one of the big shaper companies, and the car they sent for Eva used to drive around to that wing, but Grog pulled up in front of the soaring transmission tower.

"Slot one-two-oh-eight in the parking garage," he said. "Take her around for me, will you, Cormac? See you in the studio. Thanks."

At the main entrance he showed a pass to the security guard who said, "Hi, Grog, nice morning . . . hey, is this Eva?" Eva shook the guard's hand and followed Grog through the huge hallway to the elevators. At the hundred-and-somethingth floor the elevator voice said "Terminus. Terminus. Upper floors not yet open." Grog slid a plastic card into a slot, and the elevator went on up.

"Okay," he said as it slowed. "I want to carry you this bit. Shut your eyes. Don't open them till I say so, or you'll spoil the fun. Huh! You're heavier than I guessed!"

Mystified, Eva closed her eyes and clung. She heard the doors open and smelled food-smells. Grog's footsteps made no noise on a thick carpet. He stopped and she heard the faint flip of switches, then the hum of a shaper-zone warming— more than one, and huge, making her fur creep with static. The hum died as the zones settled into their shapes.

"Okay, you can look now," said Grog.

She opened her eyes and saw jungle—dark, rich greenness, swaying faintly. Now the noises began, rustles, birdcalls, a weird distant howling, the splash of water. But no smells, only yesterday's food. An enormous orange spider scuttled across the brown dead leaves toward Grog's feet, and vanished. It wasn't real. It had just reached the edge of the zone. She turned her head and over Grog's shoulder saw a table and chairs, and a little way off another one in another gap in the zones; then another and another; and then, farther off still, daylight, the brilliant sky over the city, seen through big windows high up in the building.

"Uh?" she grunted.

"Executive restaurant," said Grog. "Center of the world, kind of. The fat bastards who decide what we're all going to see and think sit in their offices and look at the instant-feedback figures and then they come up here and fight out over their steaks what we're going to see and think next. They can't do a vital job like that without something pretty to look at in the background, can they? Want something else?"

He pressed a key on the control box he was carrying and they were on a paved square in Venice, under striped umbrellas, with palaces and gondolas around; a moment later they were under palms on an island, with blue-green waves breaking into surf. He brought the jungle back.

"It's not even tape," he said. "It's real. This very minute, out in Cayamoro, that snake's looking for tree frogs."

The snake was pale green, with a dark stripe along its spine. Eva felt herself shudder at the sight of it. She almost jumped back into Grog's arms. She hadn't minded snakes when she'd been human—not on the shaper anyway. Now it was Kelly's impulse, barely controllable, to leap away and chatter her fright. Teeth bared, she watched the snake slide out of sight. It took her a minute or two more to gather the courage to explore.

Of course Eva had seen jungle on the shaper at home, but there the zone filled only a part of the living room, less than life-size. You could walk into it, but it was all so crowded that you couldn't help walking through the shapes, and you felt huge, and you could see out all around to the same old walls and chairs and pictures. This was different. It was almost real, apart from the tables and chairs. Faint marks on the floor showed the narrow pathways between the zones where the guests and the waiters came and went, but on either side you seemed to peer deep into living jungle, succulent leaves, shaggy peeling bark with yellow berries. A hummingbird darted across a space, its wings a blur, emerald mist. Beneath the leaf litter something moved, emerged, jet-black, a millipede twenty centimeters long. Between two trunks stretched a strange white vague thing; small yellow spiders scuttled through it, hundreds of them; it was their communal web; when a moth blundered in they were on their victim in a flash. All around was a sense of danger. Could you eat the berries, the bugs, the leaves? Was the millipede deadly? Or the snake?

But along with the danger was excitement, yearning. This was where you belonged. This was Kelly's dream.

Eventually she knuckled her way back and found Grog standing by one of the wide windows, staring south.

"Uh?" she said.

"Going to see the real thing," he said. "I'm flying out to Cayamoro, day after tomorrow."

"Uh?"

"Just have a look around. Size things up. People too."

You couldn't just go to Cayamoro like that. But Grog could. He held up a finger.

"Hear that?" he said.

The far faint wail had begun again.

"Howler monkey," he said. "Jungle should be full of that noise, but they got their figures wrong when they set it all up. The howler population's gone down and down. They're not going to survive. So there's room for a new big ape in Cayamoro."

Eva understood at once what he was talking about. She was surprised. Surely he'd learned enough by now.

"We wouldn't survive either," she said. "It's been tried."

"No, it hasn't. Not what I've in mind."

"Have you told Dad? First time we met, I said ask him."

"Said as much as I could, short of getting slung out of the door. Not a good listener, your dad. You've got to remember he's got a whole lot of his life tied up in the Pool. One thing I've learned is we're going to have a tougher time educating humans than we are educating chimps."

"It's been tried."

"Sure—I've read the literature, Stella Brewer, for instance, great girl, trying to teach chimps how to live in the wild after they'd been used for learning experiments, lived in houses, worn clothes, eaten off plates."

"I thought some of hers were wild."

"Yeah. Brought in as babies by poachers, and some of them she won with, too—just a few. None of that matters. All I know is we've got to try again. We can't go on as we are. You've been born with the Pool, Eva, grown up with it. It's an always-there thing for you. But it isn't. The way things are going, in twenty years' time the Pool will be finished."

"Uh!"

"I've seen the figures. To you, being short of funds is just another always-there thing, but it's been getting worse. There's a trend. It started long before you were born. I'm not just talking about the Pool and I'm not just talking about money. It's happening all over. The whole human race is thinking in shorter and shorter terms. The bright kids aren't going into research; the investors aren't putting their money into anything that doesn't give them a quick return; governments and institutions aren't funding basic research; we're pulling back from space exploration—you name it, we're doing it. We're giving up. Packing it in."

"Uh?"

"Trouble with us humans is we keep forgetting we're animals. You know what happens when an animal population expands beyond what the setup will bear? Nature finds ways of cutting them back. Usually it's plain starvation, but even when there's food to go around something gets triggered inside them. They stop breeding or they eat their own babies or peck one another to death—there's all sorts of ways. Us too. It's in us. We can't escape it. A lot of it's been going on already for years without anyone noticing, a sort of retreat, a backing out, nine-tenths of the world's population holed up in their apartments twenty-four hours a day watching the shaper. But it's starting to move. I can feel it. There's a real crash coming, and us being humans, whatever it is, we're going to overdo it. You know what that means for you chimps? Lana's children, or her children's children, are going to have to fend for themselves. You think they'll make it out there?"

He flicked his head toward the endless vista of high rises, veiled in their human haze.

"Not a hope," he said. "They've got to be somewhere

where there's trees to shelter them, leaves that come and
come, fruit all year round, small game—the life they were
made for."

"They've forgotten."

"They'll have to learn all over . . . No, listen . . ."

He had gripped her hand as she stretched it over the keyboard.

". . . there's chances now. There's something new, something Brewer and the others didn't have. When they tried to
teach chimps how to live wild, they had one big problem—
they were human. They couldn't lead, they could only push
—push the chimps out into a world where humans didn't fit.
It makes your heart bleed, how they tried, the things they
gave up. But you could lead, Eva."

"Uh!"

"You and the others. Stefan's due to wake up, any day
now."

"Uh?"

"Chimp used to be called Caesar. Yasha's a month behind.
Then there'll be three of you."

Eva had not asked about Caesar since the night of her tantrum, and Mom and Dad hadn't mentioned him either,
though Mom was probably hoping that when Joan's other pa-
tients began to awaken, to become available for company,
then Eva would stop wanting to spend so much time at the
Reserve. Eva wasn't sure what she felt about this. Some ways
it would be good to know chimps who could also talk—bitch
about friends, discuss music, tease, plan lives—but she had
now discovered other kinds of talk, in glance and gesture and
especially touch, that gave her everything she needed.

"What do you think you're *for*?" said Grog.

"Uh?"

"Yeah. What are you *for*, Eva? What's your purpose? Are
you just a freak? Are you just here so Professor Pradesh can

prove things about neuron memory? 'Course, that's why the old girl chimped you, but do you reckon it's enough? Are you happy with just that? Being a scientific curiosity and selling drinks on the shaper? Listen. Your dad and the people who helped chimp you did it for their own reasons, and your mom said yes to save your life. They didn't know the real reason. The real reason was that you and Stefan and the others are the ones who are going to show the chimps how to survive. Nature doesn't like letting species go. She's going to save the chimps if she can, and that's why she let you happen.''

Eva stared. She would hardly have known him. He stood in the brilliant morning light with the shaper jungle behind him, hunched, pop-eyed, quivering with the energies of his argument. She fluttered her fingers across the keys to tell him he was crazy. His whole idea was doubly impossible. You couldn't teach chimps to live on their own, not any longer. You couldn't persuade people to let you try. But try to tell Grog that. He simply wouldn't understand. He was like his mother in one of her rages, an unstoppable force, blind with his passion. She canceled the words and just grunted doubt.

"Yeah," he said. "It'll take a bit of thinking about. Don't expect you to give me a yes right off. It's a long-term project— five years minimum. We've got to make a whole world see reason. They will in the end—they've got no other choice. But for you, Eva, do you want this . . .''

He waved a hand at the green compelling jungle.

''. . . or this?''

He pressed keys. The jungle whipped away and the restaurant was filled with ruins, part of a dead city under gray moonlight with gray and grassless hills rimming the horizon—not real, part of a set for some shaper epic probably, but eerie, not just because of the sense of ghostliness and loss but because of the way the tables and chairs stood among the broken walls and rubble-littered floors, waiting and waiting for guests who would never come.

"Time to go," said Grog. "Got to keep on my mother's good side—we're going to need her."

MONTH EIGHT,
DAY TWENTY-NINE

Living with the dream . . .
Imaginary trees filling the iron grove . . .
Shadows, leaf litter, looping creepers, the flash of a
 bird . . .
Calls, whispers, odors . . .

A card had come from Grog that morning, saying he was staying a week longer because he'd picked up some kind of jungle
bug, but the picture of Cayamoro was more beautiful than
anything she'd ever seen. So now as she played with Abel she
did so absentmindedly, making imaginary scenarios of escape
not just for herself but for Lana and Beth and the rest of them
—putting something in their food that would send them all to
sleep, and flying them south and then letting them wake,
amazed, among the odors and shadows they were made
for . . .

A shriek! Lana! Another! Eva scuttled around the corner of
the concrete slab against which she'd been leaning. Lana was
lying flat on her face on the ground with a male chimp jumping on her. Beth and Dinks were watching, shrieking too, with
all their teeth showing, outraged but too scared to help. Wang
was actually under Lana, squealing each time the weight of
the male came down. The male had his back to Eva. She flung
herself at him, leaping at the last instant to crash into his
spine while he was actually in the middle of a jump. He probably weighed twice what she did, but he wasn't ready and she
knocked him flat on his face, then raced on around the corner

of the concrete slab, and the next corner too. There was just a chance he hadn't even seen her and wouldn't know what had happened. The shrieks on the other side of the slab became deafening. The male appeared, actually above her head, half crouching on the slab, screaming back at the females on the other side. Eva bit him on the ankle as hard as she could. He raced away, swung himself up the nearest iron tree, and clung there, shrieking. It had all happened in about fifteen seconds.

Eva peered out to see if Lana was all right and found Lana, Beth, Dinks, and another female grouped at the bottom of the iron tree and screaming up at the male. Eva went over and joined the racket. It was extremely satisfying, having a big male cornered like that and telling him to come down if he dared. With another part of her mind she worked out what had happened, though to the real chimps it was all so ordinary they had no need to think about it.

Dad had told Eva the set-up before she'd first joined, and part of her "work" for him—her excuse for being at the Reserve—was keeping him up-to-date with the latest moves. Beth's little "family"—Dad called it a subgroup—was part of a larger group that contained two adult males. Tatters, the one up the tree now, was the stronger, but Geronimo was older and had been boss of the group for several years while Tatters was still growing up. Now Tatters was challenging him. Tatters would have won a straight fight easily enough, but Geronimo had the females on his side. Beth, in particular, supported him, partly because she was used to him but partly because having the boss on her side helped her to dominate the younger females. Geronimo made a point of going around the female subgroups and sitting grooming with each of them. Tatters's latest move in the contest was trying to break this alliance up by attacking any females who paid attention to Geronimo. Presumably he'd seen Lana and Geronimo grooming before Eva had arrived that morning, so he'd tried to punish her. He hadn't seriously hurt her. There were rules. Males never used their terrifying teeth to bite females, though they did sometimes with other males. He might possibly have killed Wang, but that would have been an accident. Certainly he wouldn't have expected a surprise ambush by a single female—that wasn't in the rules. If he worked out what had happened, Eva guessed, she'd be in for a rough time.

Now, attracted by the uproar, Geronimo came rambling over, with a young male called Sniff who tended to follow Geronimo around. Geronimo settled onto a slab with his back toward the tree. As soon as Beth noticed him she came over and greeted him with quick submissive bows and pants. He looked around in a lordly way and pretended to notice Tatters in the tree for the first time. Beth settled beside him and began to groom him. Dinks came over and presented her rump to him and then joined in grooming the other side. The three females left at the foot of the tree didn't feel confident enough to go on shrieking at Tatters without the support of Beth and Dinks, so they backed off and settled down together. Eva put her arm around Lana to comfort her for her bad treatment, while Lana began to inspect Wang for signs of damage. Wang was trembling with fright and stared at the world with shining, baffled eyes.

There would be cameras running up in the observation posts, and students taking notes, but they were all outside the story. Eva was inside it. She could feel little Wang's fright and Lana's quick recovery to her usual contented self. She could feel too that Lana hadn't seen how she'd been rescued. When Geronimo slowly turned to look up at Tatters, still grinning in the iron tree, and raised a beckoning hand to him, inviting him down, Eva could sense both the mockery in the gesture and the genuine suggestion of peacemaking. Tatters stayed where he was. His teeth still gleamed inside his tight-drawn lips, showing he was worried and nervous, though the threat

from the females had gone. Perhaps, Eva thought, he was baffled by what had happened; at one moment he'd been fully in
control, winning, punishing Lana, with the others too scared
to interfere, and the next moment he'd been flat on his face,
harried by the females, bitten and chased up a tree.

Eva studied all this with quick, secret glances. It took her a
little time to realize that she herself was being watched, by
Sniff. He was sitting alone, a few yards off, with his head
bowed as if lost in some private dream, but his eyes were
darting from side to side. The moment Eva caught his glance
he looked away. This happened two or three times, until she
realized that Sniff was actually doing much the same that she
was, watching deliberately in order to learn how things
worked. The moment he realized that she'd been staring at
him, he turned his back on her.

The wild thought struck her that Sniff was actually like
her, another chimp with a human mind, whom Dad hadn't
told her about. No, impossible. Everything that had happened
from her first waking, right through to the things people said
during her checkups in Joan's lab, made her certain she was
the only one. So far.

At last Tatters came down from the tree and ambled off.
Lana was feeling extra possessive about Wang, and Dinks and
Beth were still busy with Geronimo, but Abel, who'd been
frightened enough by the fight to go and nestle against Beth's
side, became restless again, so Eva took him off to continue
their game. This consisted of a variation on the original trick
with the bottle and cord, which allowed Eva sometimes to tie
him a loose knot and when it came undone to see if he could
be persuaded to try and retie it himself. At first he'd just held
the ends together and hoped and then brought it to Eva to
mend, but she had refused to retie the knot unless he sat and
watched what she was doing. Now when it came apart he'd

gotten as far as twisting the ends together before giving up—anything like a real knot was still an accident.

They were sitting together, Eva knotting the loose ends with clear, exaggerated movements, and Abel peering with his nose so close to her fingers that it looked as if he were trying to understand the process by smell, when she felt a faint movement against her shoulder. She looked around and saw Sniff crouching just behind her, watching what she was doing. He backed away at once, but she turned and gave him a quick pant of greeting, then finished tying the knot and gave the toy to Abel, who scampered away, trailing it behind him.

Sniff sat gazing at her. He was an odd-looking chimp with a shorter, squarer face than most and large pale ears. He wasn't quite full grown, but Eva had the impression that even when he was he still wouldn't be as big as Tatters or Geronimo. He faced her with a bright, steady stare, challenging and inquisitive. She was aware at once that he had realized she was different. He wanted to know why.

This was new to Eva. Most of the chimps she'd met probably vaguely realized there was something a little strange about her, but didn't distinguish Eva's kind of oddity from the oddities of some of the other chimps—Lulu's deafness or Gran's refusal to mate, ever. She panted again and moved up beside him, but when she started to groom him he took her hand in his and studied it carefully, back and front, before letting go. Then he picked up a short piece of the cord she'd been using and gave it to her. She knotted the two ends, showing him every move and passed him the resultant loop, which he stared at for a while, then took in two fists and tore apart. The cord broke at a weakness, but the knot stayed tied. Sniff was still staring at it when a new hullabaloo broke out behind the slab. Together they rose and peered over the top.

Tatters had come back. Eva could see the back of his head and shoulders with his hair all bushed out as he swayed and stamped to and fro, hooting softly. Beth and Dinks, out of sight, were shrieking at him. Eva knuckled around to the corner of the slab to watch the whole scene. Geronimo had actually turned his back on Tatters, trying to pretend he wasn't there, but Beth and Dinks had stopped grooming to watch Tatters and shriek. Tatters was an alarming sight. With his hair bushed out and his ponderous stamping movements, he managed to make himself look even larger and heavier than he really was. The rhythm of his stamping increased. Dinks noticed Eva and held out a beseeching hand—"Come and help." Eva turned her head to look for Lana, who was out of sight, so she started forward to join the others, but before she reached them Tatters charged, not directly at Geronimo but between him and Beth, knocking them both over. He swung his charge into a circling movement, and finding Eva directly in his path he slapped her aside, sending her head over heels. She screeched and rose with her head ringing. The slap had been a terrific buffet, but it hadn't actually hurt all that much. Still, it was an outrage. Geronimo was on his feet now, screeching too, a little uncertainly, but with Beth and Dinks beside him he gathered the courage to rush at Tatters. Lana had appeared from somewhere and joined in, so Eva did too. Together they drove Tatters up the tree again. Sniff, Eva noticed, did nothing, but watched the whole episode from a few yards off.

Twenty minutes later, at Geronimo's invitation, Tatters came down and this time the two males settled down to an intensive grooming session, totally absorbed, locked into each other's arms. This was perfectly ordinary. It was the way most fights ended. It was even ordinary that a little later when Eva had started her game with Abel again, Beth came ambling past and seemed to notice her. She stared a moment, puzzled, and then without warning rushed at Eva and bit her hard on the shoulder. Eva shrieked—the bite hurt a good deal more than the buffet from Tatters. Abel raced off. Lana came over, beginning to shriek too, but instead of continuing the fight Beth knuckled rapidly away, leaving Lana to comfort Eva and lick the bite mark, which had actually drawn blood. Eva sat trembling with shock, but she knew she shouldn't have been surprised. Beth must have seen the attack on Tatters and known what had happened; and though she had joined in driving Tatters up the tree, she still couldn't approve of a junior female acting with that kind of initiative. So as soon as she'd recovered from her shakes, Eva went and found Beth and gave her a very formal submissive bow and pant, just to keep things straight. Beth, of course, pretended not to notice but was clearly pleased. This was something Eva could see and feel, but the researchers in the observation posts couldn't, though they'd have most of the other details of the fight recorded.

Right at the end of Eva's visit something much more extraordinary happened. She took her chance to slip away and knuckled over to the door she used. A short wall screened it from the rest of the area. The door itself was a heavy metal thing with an observation grill in it and a lock humans could operate and chimps couldn't—a box with a tricky catch and inside it a four-digit code to punch. Eva had slipped through and was putting on her overalls when she heard a movement and glanced up. Four chimp fingers were gripped into the grill. Quickly Eva switched the light off. The square of daylight blanked out, and now Eva could see the gleam of eyes and the pale muzzle pressed against the bars of the grill. Though she couldn't recognize him, she knew it could only be Sniff. He hung there for some time before he dropped away. She heard him trying the catch and then thumping the box itself, not in a violent frustrated way as Tatters might have done, but more experimentally, to see if a good thump opened it.

Eva finished dressing in the dark, picked up her voice box and stole away. A last glance back showed her Sniff peering in at the grill once more. The observers would have noted his behavior, she realized. She'd have to discuss it with Dad. Pity. It was something she felt an instinct to keep to herself for the moment. She didn't know why.

MONTH NINE, DAY FOURTEEN

Living in the real world . . .
No dreams, only people.
Rush and crush.
Winter again, soon.

Eva made a tape to take to Grog in the hospital. On one side
she put the reasons why she wasn't going to help him in his
campaign to get the chimps moved to Cayamoro. Long arguments like that she usually put on tape, because it took so
long to spell them out face-to-face. She had plenty of reasons
—reasons to do with chimps. (How could you let chimps
loose in wild jungle when they didn't know a poisonous berry
from a safe one, or what a leopard was? How could you cope
with males like Tatters and Geronimo? How could you hope
for any of them to follow Eva's lead, so junior, such an outsider? And so on.) Reasons to do with humans. (How would
you raise the funds? How would you persuade people like Dad
to stop what they were doing? How would you get the people
who looked after Cayamoro to let you put a lot of chimps in
their jungle? And so on.) Eva's own reasons . . .

She found these harder to get said, but she had to, to be fair
to Grog. She was happy with things as they were. Perhaps
happy was the wrong word, but she felt she'd reached a balance she could live with. She needed human company as well
as chimp company. She needed Ginny and Bren in the same
sort of way she needed Lana. She enjoyed human things—

cooked food, surfboarding, travel. She'd be going skiing in a couple of months. It wasn't fair to ask her to give all that up.

Or to have to tell Mom she was going to go away and live in Cayamoro and never see her again.

Eva played the tape through to check. It was all right, firm, and final . . . but poor Grog. She turned the tape over and filled the other side with chitchat about things that had happened while he'd been away and then ill—the fight with Tatters, Mom's most tiresome client winning a lottery, Sniff, Mimi's latest rage, Abel's first real knot, and so on. Bright bedside prattle. It was so difficult to imagine Grog being ill. Almost dying, apparently.

Mimi had chartered an air ambulance and flown out and brought him back to the university hospital, but he'd been too ill for visitors. Eva had called again, because she was due in for her monthly check at Joan Pradesh's lab, and again she'd been told no, but then the hospital had called back to say Grog was asking for her, but she mustn't stay more than five minutes. It sounded as though he must still be pretty bad. Even so, she wasn't ready for the shock.

All his hair had fallen out. His face was the color of the underside of a fish, with all the flesh wasted from beneath the skin. His eyes were dull, yellow, exhausted, but at least they moved. If he'd had them shut, she would have thought he was dead. She realized at once she couldn't give him the tape.

"Hi," he whispered. "Good to see you."

"Uh?" she grunted.

"Had a bad time. My fault. They thought I was done for, but they've got it licked at last. I've had half a million little wrigglers playing lurkie-lurkie around my bloodstream, but they've all gone now. Taught me a lesson. Can't send chimps to Cayamoro. Don't have the immunities any more than I had."

He closed his eyes. Eva grunted agreement and relief. He didn't notice the relief.

"Going to have to make our own jungle," he said. "Nice, clean jungle. On an island, uh?"

With the closed eyes and the whisper it was as if he were talking in his sleep, muttering his dreams. Eva mumbled sounds of doubt. His eyes opened.

"You're against?" he said.

"Uh."

"Why? Only thing makes sense."

"Tell you when you're stronger."

"No. Now."

For the first time there was a sort of energy in his eyes, a glimmer of the Grog she knew before.

"Isn't time now. I did you a tape. Give it to you later."

"Let's have it now. Come on. Listen, this is the only thing I think about. You got reasons, I want to listen to them, think about them. You've as good as told me you're anti—you can't just leave it at that. Right?"

His voice was more than a whisper now, and there was a tinge of pink in his cheeks. It was as if the argument were actually good for him. Eva took the tape out.

"Okay," she said. "I'm sorry, Grog. Listen to side one when you're feeling stronger. Side two is just talk."

"Thanks."

He closed his eyes and sighed. Eva thought he'd fallen asleep, but then his lips moved.

"Have some grapes. More than I can eat."

It was, too, a huge mound, purple and green. She took a whole bunch and felt her mouth starting to water. Grog smiled.

"Can't promise you they aren't poisoned," he said. "Mother keeps sending them."

Eva had discovered quite a human-sounding chuckle she

could do with her own mouth, but she couldn't control it the way she could her voice-box remarks, so now it came out all false.

Her sense of shock and depression deepened as she knuckled along corridors and rode escalators and elevators to Joan's lab. Checkups had, in any case, become rather boring by now. Nothing new was likely to happen, so Joan left them to her assistants. They wired you up and made you run on a moving belt and do other kinds of exercises; then, still wired up, you did memory tests and perception tests and intelligence tests; then they showed you shapings of things that were supposed to stir you up in different ways—human and chimp babies, a car crash, a snake eating a mouse, a nude male model, a bowl of apples, and so on, while the machines you were wired to recorded your pulse and your palm moisture and your brain rhythms and dozens of other things happening inside you and fed the results into computers to be juggled around. Today, by the time she reached this stage the shapings seemed to mean nothing at all.

"Are you okay, sweetie?" said Minnie. She was a happy, round-faced girl with a sharp little nose and tiny eyes. She was far brighter than she looked, Eva had found.

"Uh?"

"Only you hardly seem to be registering."

"Sorry. Thinking about something else."

Just saying so brought back the image of Grog, bald and beardless on the pillow.

"Whup!" said Minnie. "Something registered there!"

"I visited a friend on the way. He's been very ill. All his hair's fallen out."

"Too bad."

"Chimps mind about hair."

"So you do too?"

"Uh."

"Okay. Let's see if we can find you something nice and shaggy."

Minnie pressed keys. The computer thought for an instant, then came up with a ridiculous dog, a girl in a woolly suit, a bottle brush, a caterpillar, a diatom, a college professor. They began to laugh and were still laughing when Joan Pradesh came in. She glanced scornfully at the professor.

"An utter charlatan," she said. "How's it going, Minnie?"

"She's not been concentrating. She's a bit upset. She's been visiting a sick friend."

Joan nodded, not interested. She took over the console from Minnie and whizzed through the earlier results, faster than you'd have thought anyone could have taken them in.

"Absolutely normal," she said. "I think we can stop doing this—we are not going to get anything new. Of course, I am not a psychologist—I can judge only the physiological data. Do you feel yourself to be a fully integrated creature, Eva?"

"Most of the time. Only I get chimp urges I've got to go along with. I'm more chimp than you expected, aren't I?"

Joan said nothing, but stared at the VDU, not really seeing it. She rose.

"We'll disconnect her now, Minnie," she said.

"We haven't quite finished."

"Never mind."

Joan helped remove the sensors with quick and expert fingers. She might be arrogant, but she wasn't proud.

"Now, come with me," she said and led the way out into the corridor and along to a windowless room, one wall of which was lined with VDUs. Meg was sitting at one of the consoles. She turned and said, "Hi, Eva," but her smile was strained and sad.

"I want you to look at something," said Joan. "I'm not going to tell you about it because I don't want to put ideas into your head. If you find it too distressing, you must tell me.''

She pressed a switch. A zone hummed, and at the other end of the room shapes became solid—a hospital bed ringed by machines, the broken web, the thing like a hairy spider at the center—a chimp's head on the pillow, split by a huge, strain-ing grin. The gleaming canines showed it was a male. The eyes were wide open, staring at the ceiling.

Eva knuckled across to the zone and circled it. So this was what was left of the boy called Stefan and the chimp called Caesar. It could only be them. She felt her lips beginning to strain in sympathy, copying the grin of horror.

To Dad's surprise and Mom's relief Eva had not wanted to talk much about what would happen when Joan's new pa-tients woke. People expected her to be excited at the idea of having companions like herself, but her own feelings were more mixed. There had even been a strand of jealousy in them, at the knowledge that soon she would be losing her own uniqueness. Fame was funny. You didn't want to share it. But much more important than that had been the fear, half thought and half felt, that having others like her would upset the balance she had achieved. Because there was no one like her, people had to accept her as human when she was with them, just as the chimps accepted her as chimp when she was in the Reserve. When the others came, wouldn't people, even Ginny and Bren, find it harder not to think of her as *other*, different and unwanted? And Eva herself, would she still want to be with Lana as much as she did? That was something too precious to lose, but you couldn't keep it alive just by wanting to. So on the whole, Eva had not spent much time thinking about the moment when she would first meet Stefan/Caesar. Perhaps that was why, when the moment came, the shock was not the simple selfish shock of disappointment. It was pure shock, shock at the thing itself.

The bedclothes beside the body moved.

"Erch," said a voice. "Gningg."

Eva knuckled back to Joan.

"Something wrong?" she said.

"We began the resuscitation procedure nineteen days ago. We had earlier felt able to take a few shortcuts on the basis of what we learned from you, and it is just possible that we made a mistake there, but if so, it hasn't shown up in any of our tests. Personally I am confident that the transfer has taken place, that Stefan's axon network has replicated in the animal's brain, that he is, in lay terms, *there.* But for some reason he is unable to communicate, either with the animal's body or through it with the outside world."

Eva turned and circled the zone again, staring at the image on the image bed. No use.

"Can I go in?" she said.

"If you don't mind going through the sterilizer."

"You won't have to do my clothes."

Eva stripped and stood in the little cubicle. Her hair bushed out around her under the tingling bombardment. She opened the inner door and went through. The room was just the same as when she used to lie here, with the bed and the mirror and the silent machines, and beyond the window the huge sky with the city stretching away beneath it. She pulled a stool over to the bed and climbed on to it, so that she could lean over and peer down into the dark eyes. There was nothing she could read there, no presence, no signal. Her hand moved without her telling it to and began to groom through the long black hairs on the scalp.

"He hasn't got any feeling there," said Meg's voice. "Just his left arm and his mouth."

Eva shifted the bedclothes back. The hand lay across a keyboard just like hers. Sometimes the fingers twitched, and when they touched the "Speak" bar a voice came out, mean-

ingless. She settled herself and started to groom her way pains-
takingly up the arm. Was there a faint response, felt through
her fingertips, as though the flesh itself recognized the signal?
But when she peered into the eyes again she saw no change,
and the agonized grin stayed tense.

She lifted the twitching fingers aside and pressed the keys.

"Hi," said a boy's voice from the keyboard speaker. "I'm
Stefan. I'm here. I'm okay."

The arm threshed at the sound, straining against the straps
that held it.

"That is his regular reaction," said Joan out of the air. "Violent agitation."

Eva let the threshings subside and returned to grooming the
arm. The response she imagined she had felt before was there
no longer. There was no change in the dreadful grimace, no
glimmer of any kind in the eye. After about ten minutes
Joan's voice spoke again.

"He's had as much as he can stand for the moment. Meg's
going to put him to sleep."

Eva grunted but continued her work. She wanted him to go
back into darkness with the feel of her fingers on his flesh. It
seemed important, but she didn't know why. She felt the
change in her fingertips and looked up in time to see the eyes
close, the lips lose their tension, soften, and close, too, until
the face was that of a young male chimp, asleep, deep in a
dream—a dream, perhaps, of trees.

Totally exhausted, Eva knuckled out into the control room
and put on her overalls. She was very shivery. While she had
been in the bedroom she had been too busy, too absorbed in
trying to make contact, to understand quite what she had seen
and felt. Now the horror of it gathered inside her and exploded into a howling hoot. She rocked herself to and fro in
her misery. Joan stood watching, bright-eyed, but Meg jumped

off her chair, knelt down, and cuddled beside her, sobbing with human grief.

Eva recovered first and reached for her keyboard.

"Sorry," she said. "Couldn't help it."

"We are all somewhat shaken," said Joan. "Do you have any ideas?"

"They're both there. They don't want each other."

"Both?"

"Stefan. Caesar. Like Kelly's here."

She tapped herself on the chest.

"I made myself want Kelly," she said. "I knew I had to. Suppose it's easier for me. Always been used to chimps."

"I'm afraid that may well be the answer," said Joan. "At a very early age, thanks to your father's decision to bring you up in such close contact with the Pool, you may well have learned to think of yourself as actually being a chimpanzee as well as a human, and that deep in your unconscious mind you still do so. The attraction of this theory is that the level at which rejection of the transfer is most likely to occur is very close to the unconscious, the boundary where the human mind has to mesh with the autonomous systems of the animal host."

The zone had not been switched off. Eva knuckled over and circled it, staring at the thing on the bed. She had her horror under control now, but if anything it was stronger than before. Before, she had simply felt it, in her shivers, in her howling, but now she thought it too. These humans, they couldn't know. They cared, they were sad, but they couldn't understand. This was what humans did to animals, one way or another. This was what they'd always done. The ghastly little wrigglers that had invaded Grog's bloodstream had more right to be there than Stefan had to be in Caesar, or Eva herself in Kelly.

She grunted and turned to Joan.

"So I'm going to be the only one?" she said.

"What do you mean?"

"Nobody else has been brought up with chimps."

"That is only one theory. In any case, we shall have to see."

"You're going to do *more*?"

"Sasha is due to wake in eleven days, and I shall certainly explore the possibilities of further experiments. We cannot let it rest there. But first I think we must have a session with Dr. Alonso and the animal psychology team—your father too, of course . . ."

Eva didn't go straight to the parking lot—Cormac had a new comic book so he wouldn't mind waiting. She rode elevators and scuttled along corridors until she had found her way back to Grog's room. He was lying as she'd left him, with his eyes closed. The tape was running.

". . . then what about all the people down at Cayamoro?" her voice was saying. "The scientists, for instance. They're . . ."

She crossed the room silently and switched it off. Grog opened his eyes.

"I've changed my mind," she said. "We've got to try. I'll help you."

YEAR TWO,
MONTH THREE,
DAY SEVENTEEN

Living with a purpose.
Waking with it already at work in your mind.
Allies, enemies, schemes, failures.
Secrets.
Even in the minute-by-minute life of the Reserve, thinking
  all the time.
One day . . . somehow . . .

By the time Grog's beard was long enough to groom again he could sit up, write letters, talk for an hour at a time. At the request of Stefan's parents, Joan Pradesh had put Stefan back into coma and let him stay there. There had been the girl called Sasha and a chimp called Angel. Joan's team had let them wake with their whole mouth working, and they had screamed all the time they were awake. They had done this for nine days, and then they had died.

It was supposed to be a secret, but Eva had told Grog and Grog had told a reporter he knew (of course). There was going to be a press conference this evening. The university was very jumpy about it because it was pretty well certain Joan would put everyone's back up and then sponsors would get scared and funds would be cut. So they'd arranged for Eva to be there too, clever, famous, popular Eva, the whole world's favorite cuddly toy—if Eva told people it was all right, then the fuss would die down and the funds would go on rolling in and that was all that mattered in the world . . .

"You don't need to worry," Grog had said. "There'll be

quite a few people on our side down in the audience—I've been rounding them up. If it doesn't come up some other way Mike will ask you a direct question . . ."

"Uh?"

"You'll know him—a blind white blob. Get a few lines ready on your tape. Be nice about Joan. After that, just play it by ear. This is our first big chance, but don't let that scare you. They all love you out here, remember."

Eva was trying not to think about it because it was a waste of her morning in the Reserve. Though she spent every spare minute she had here now, it still wasn't enough—not just because she was happier here, more herself, either. In fact, that wasn't true. Visits to the Reserve were sometimes very unsatisfactory, difficult or boring or frightening, harder to control than human life. And human life was a lot of fun, often exciting and interesting, and easier every day as people got used to her . . .

But that was all beside the point. She needed to be at the Reserve more, for the purpose. Suppose the impossible came true and Grog found a place where they could go and together they persuaded Dad and the others to let them, to help them when they got there, and all the other parts of the dream slotted in, what would be the use if the chimps themselves weren't ready? You couldn't tell *them* what was going to happen, teach them how to cope, any of that, so "ready" just meant trusting Eva, being prepared to follow her lead—an outsider, a female, a juvenile, coming and going at random. Not easy.

Winter had been tough. Some days the chimps hardly went out into the open at all but stayed in their "caves" squabbling for places nearest the heated patches of wall and floor. In those close unnatural quarters tempers were bad, and the signals for keeping them in control didn't always work. Tatters and Geronimo had several real fights, with serious bite wounds. By the end of the winter Tatters was boss, which was a bad thing all around, because Geronimo used to use his authority to keep the fights among the females from getting serious, by siding with the one who looked as if she was losing, which was why on the whole the females had supported him, but Tatters wasn't clever enough for that. By the time the spring sun was strong enough to lounge and scratch in, the whole group was in a sour mood.

Lulu stole Wang deliberately. She must have been waiting her chance for some time, not only for Wang to get far enough away from Lana to be grabbed and run off with but also for Tatters to be somewhere near. In fact, thinking about it afterward, Eva realized that she had been half aware of Lulu sitting about a dozen paces off, watching Beth's group most of the time but also glancing over her shoulder as if looking for something out of sight of the rest of them. They should have been aware of the danger. Lulu had never managed to rear a baby of her own because her deafness kept her from hearing the cries and whimpers that would have told her its needs, so she couldn't really be trusted near someone else's. Unfortunately Beth was in a cantankerous mood, and the other three were preoccupied with watching for a sudden attack from her. The first they knew of the kidnapping was Wang's chittering scream as Lulu dashed away, dragging him by one arm and bashing him casually against the hard ground as she went.

Lana raced after her, shrieking, with Eva close behind. They galloped around the corner of a slab and stopped dead because Tatters was there, facing them, with his hair bushed out and his face drawn into a hoot. Beth and Beth's group had supported Geronimo longer than any of the other females, and Tatters hadn't yet forgiven them. Lulu settled down behind Tatters and started grooming Wang, holding him upside down by one leg while he struggled and shrilled. Lana shrieked at Lulu until Tatters rushed at her. Eva raced in to try and grab

Wang while his back was turned, but Tatters must have seen
what she was up to, because just as she faced Lulu's snarl,
looking for an opening, she felt a stunning buffet on the side
of her head and was spun sideways across the rough concrete.
Before she could rise, Tatters landed on her with all his
weight, driving her back to the ground. The breath shrieked
out of her. As Tatters jumped to come down again she managed to wriggle sideways so that he half missed his footing,
giving her a moment to tumble herself right over into one of
the pits and out of sight. By the time Tatters realized what
had happened, she was out on the far side of the pit and
swinging up one of the iron trees.

Tatters was still full of aggression. He could easily have
followed her up the tree and continued punishing her there;
despite her advantage of being uppermost he would have been
much too quick and strong for her, but that was against the
rules. He swung around looking for another target. Lulu was
crouched where she'd been, licking a bite wound on her arm
and moaning between licks. Wang had gone, and so had Lana,
but Geronimo had been sitting all this while (about twenty
seconds) with his back to the squabble, pretending not to
know it was happening, while Sniff had been perched a little
farther off, as usual watching the whole scene.

Now Tatters knuckled over to Geronimo and began to circle him, hooting, with his hair bushed out. Geronimo, head
bowed, watched him out of the corner of his eye. Geronimo
had three options. He could challenge Tatters back or he
could submit by bowing down and panting and letting Tatters
step over him or he could run away up a tree. The tension
mounted. Any moment now, he would make a dash for it. But
then an odd thing happened. Sniff rose, came over, settled by
Geronimo, and put his arm around him. Geronimo looked at
him. Tatters, absorbed in his aggression display, seemed not to
notice what had happened until he had circled completely

around the pair and come face-to-face again. By this time they were standing. Their hair rose like Tatters's. They hooted. Geronimo took a half pace forward. Tatters stopped dead in his tracks and looked away. Geronimo hooted again. Tatters hesitated, turned, and knuckled away. Geronimo and Sniff settled down to groom each other.

Waiting till Tatters was safely out of sight, Eva climbed down the tree, but Sniff must have been watching her, because he instantly left Geronimo and came across to meet her. Eva hadn't seen much of Sniff during the winter. According to the human observers, he'd gone off and joined up with a different group in one of the other ruined factories while Tatters and Geronimo were fighting it out, so it didn't seem like him to have behaved as he had just done, especially since he was intelligent enough to know that Tatters would make him pay for it as soon as he could get him alone. Now he looked at Eva gravely. She stayed where she was while he went around and gave her rump a quick sniff, then returned to peer into her eyes again. He grunted quietly to himself, then put out a hand and patted her twice gently, on the side of the cheek. It was not a signal she had ever seen one chimp give another, but she understood at once what it meant. "Don't worry. I'll look after you." He grunted again and went back to Geronimo.

Later that morning Tatters came charging into Beth's group, buffeting them aside and rushing away before they could join up to drive him off. Apart from that, nothing much happened until it was time for Eva to leave. She found Sniff sitting in the little nook that screened the door. She paused. The obvious thing would have been to greet him briefly and move on, as though she were passing by on her way to somewhere else, but she could see from his whole pose and the sudden alertness at her arrival that he had been waiting for her and wouldn't be deceived.

He rose, looked at her, went to the door, and rattled the

grill, then turned and went to the box that contained the lock. He rapped it with his knuckles, looked at her sharply, and held out a hand— "Show me." All right, thought Eva, I'm going to need a male I can trust, so I'll have to let him see I trust him. She undid the catch, lifted the lid, and punched the code. Sniff watched every detail but jumped with alarm when the door lock clicked. Eva opened the door.

Grinning with nerves, Sniff peered into the darkness beyond. She switched on the light and led the way through, but he stayed close by the door, excited, frightened, his eyes darting from side to side. Now that she'd made the decision to trust him, Eva felt it was important to let him understand as much as he could, so she fetched her overalls from the peg and put them on. Though the policy at the Reserve was to keep humans out of sight as much as possible, from time to time they had to intervene in one way or another, so all the chimps would have seen them. They might not understand about clothes but they'd know they had something to do with humans.

She turned and faced Sniff. He came a pace closer, put out a finger, and touched the butterfly on her chest. (This had become a sort of trademark that she always wore—in fact, a kid's clothing firm had just signed a contract to market Mom's designs worldwide, under the name of Evaralls. Apparently it was going to bring in a ton of money, both for Mom and the Pool.)

Eva always carried something to nibble, so she had a bar of raisin shortbread in the pocket; she took it out, unwrapped it, broke it in two, and gave him half. He sniffed it and peered at it before he bit and inspected the wrapping too. It was all typical, though just like any ordinary chimp he insisted on looking in the pocket to see if she had another bar. After that she sat with him by the door for a grooming session and then rose and beckoned him back out into the open. He seemed to understand exactly what was happening. Before she left him she patted his cheek, the way he'd done hers. He grunted and knuckled away without waiting for the door to close behind her.

Joan made a real hash of the press conference, worse than anybody could have guessed. She was aggressive and contemptuous, making it obvious that she despised journalists even more than she despised everyone else, and couldn't accept that they had any business to question the rightness of whatever she'd done. There was a man from the university, tall and handsome with silky white hair, who tried to smooth things out and calm everyone down and put Joan's answers into blander phrases, but he only made things worse. At least you could see Joan was being honest; she stuck her chin out and her eyes flashed and she said exactly what she thought, but the man wriggled and squirmed and tried to slither away from the point and blur everything over. Eva could see Joan becoming increasingly irritated by his efforts to tell people that she didn't really mean what she'd just been saying. Tempers were snapping, when a fat, shiny-bald young man with huge thick-lensed glasses stood up and waited for a pause in the shouting.

"Can we hear from Eva?" he said. "You have the subject of one of these experiments here. May we hear her views?"

"Well . . ." began the silky man.

"Or is she just here to look pretty?" said Mike.

"That's a very . . ." began the silky man.

Eva was sitting on a stool on the other side of Joan, but she reached out a long arm and grabbed the microphone. The man tried to snatch it back, but she was far too strong for him. There was a crackle and rasp from the speakers, and she had it. She pressed the "Speak" bar on her keyboard.

"Joan saved some of my life," said her voice. "So some of me's glad. But all of me knows she was wrong."

The silky man had left his chair and come around behind. His hand was reaching for the mike.

"I think, if you don't mind . . ."

Eva turned on him with a snarl. Her teeth snapped shut a millimeter from his wrist. He leapt away as if she'd actually bitten him. Several of the journalists cheered. Mike was still on his feet.

" 'Some of me,' " he said.

Eva climbed on to the table. She tapped her chest.

"This belongs to a chimp called Kelly," she said. "You people stole it from her. You thought you'd killed her so that you could steal it, but some of her's still here. Some of her's me. She knows what you did, so I know. I know it's wrong."

That was all she'd prepared, so she had to pause. The shouting began, everyone trying to get their questions in. The silky man reached for the microphone again, but Eva bared her teeth and he drew back. Joan looked at her and put her hand out, palm up.

"May I?" she murmured.

"You're just another monkey, remember," said Eva.

It was the gesture, like one of Lana's or Dinks's, that had put the thought into her mind, and she was really saying it only to Joan, but the mike picked the words up loud enough for everyone to hear. There was laughter and a drop in tension. Joan smiled her thin smile as she took the mike.

"Eva is almost right," she said. "I am, in fact, an ape, not a monkey, and so are chimpanzees. Eva's argument is that one species is not entitled to exploit another, one individual member of a species is not entitled even to save its own life, or the life of its child, at the expense of the life of a member of another species. I'm afraid this is nonsense. I would point out that when there were still wild chimpanzees, they hunted and ate any small monkeys they could catch, whereas for humans to eat monkeys was comparatively uncommon. Most civilized people would have regarded eating anything so human-seeming with revulsion, and among primitive peoples it was often taboo, even in areas where monkeys were common and meat a luxury. What I might call unconscious moral standards in these matters are already quite high. It is unlikely that a chimpanzee would have any such qualms. And when it comes to my own work, I, of course, recognize that I must also exercise conscious moral standards. I certainly have no right to expend the life of a member of another species on frivolities. But I have no doubt at all that I had, and have, the right to do so in order to save a human life, as I did for Eva."

She saw Eva's fingers move on the keys and paused.

"Not to save my life. Just to know."

Joan nodded.

"All right," she said, "though that is not entirely fair. I was delighted for Eva and her parents when our first transfer succeeded. Eva herself could tell you how unhappy I was about what had happened in the case of Stefan and of Sasha . . ."

"Caesar?" interrupted Eva. "Angel?"

"Who? Oh, the two chimpanzees. No, my feelings about them are different, and I would maintain quite properly so. Their lives have not been wasted. We have learned less than we hoped from them, but we might have learned a great deal and that is my justification. In this case, the knowledge might have led almost immediately to the saving or prolonging of human life, but when my father began his work with flatworms such an outcome could not have been foreseen. Flatworms are fairly primitive life-forms, and no doubt some of you would want to draw a line somewhere on the scale between them and the chimpanzees, above which it would be improper to use the animal. This makes no sense to me. I do not know how many flatworms died in the course of our experiments—the figure must have run into thousands—but I do know that not one of them died unnecessarily. By their deaths each of them minutely advanced human knowledge. Without their deaths Eva would not be here today."

As she let go of the microphone the silky man grabbed it and edged away. Still up on the table Eva sat down and huddled into herself. She felt empty, despairing, her big chance wasted. The journalists had looked at her, but they hadn't listened. They weren't interested. All most of them wanted to do was to get the conference back to the humans, to Stefan and Sasha and what had happened to them, and how ghastly it must have been for their families, and so on. "One at a time, one at a time," the silky man kept saying.

As the shouting rose Eva bowed her head. She was wearing a pair of yellow overalls, Mom's latest, lightweight because of the shaper lights, with a huge green-and-purple butterfly on the bib. The shouts and arguments—Mike and Grog's other friends were still trying to ask questions about chimp rights—had their usual effect of making her pelt prickle and bush out, so that she could feel the pressure of the overalls enclosing her. She felt like a bubble, a bubble of frustration and anger, and now the bubble seemed to be inside her, rising up, so that she had to leap to her feet and face the human pack and let the bubble burst out in one loud bark, which echoed around the room in the sudden silence.

It wasn't enough. She had to do or say something more. They were waiting. Not words, nothing human. Deliberately she let her inward urges loose. Her hands gripped the hem of her bib and dragged it up until she could nick the point of a corner tooth into the cloth. She pulled down. The hem gave. Using all her strength, she ripped the overalls apart right down to the crotch and let go. The yellow cloth crumpled around her ankles. She stepped out of the mess and knuckled away naked along the table, past Joan, past the silky man where he sat clutching the microphone, down off the table, and out of the room. Behind her she heard the trance of silence break. She did not glance back. The bay of the human pack dwindled along the corridor.

YEAR TWO, MONTH FIVE, DAY NINE

Living with human grief . . .
The wreck of half their hopes . . .
The loss, almost, of their love . . .
Sharing the wreck, the loss, the grief . . .
But living with other hopes and other loves . . .
Living with purpose.

You reach a sort of calm where you all accept that what's done's done, but there's no going back to where you were before. When Mom comes home from work you get her her vodka and orange juice and give her a hug, but you don't sit in her lap and finger through her hair while she drinks it. You listen to Dad at supper, and make encouraging grunts and ask the right questions, but you don't ask the wrong questions—nothing about the future of the Reserve, nothing about funds, nothing about Grog.

You have to learn about Grog in other ways, because you aren't allowed to see him anymore.

The morning after the press conference Ms. Callaway had come over. She had telephoned before and asked Mom and Dad to stay at home and for Eva not to go to school. She explained that by publicly criticizing Honeybear for dressing chimps up in human clothes Eva had broken important clauses in the contracts with World Fruit and SMI. They would overlook it this time, but they were going to insist on a strict code from now on about what Eva was allowed to do or say. If she broke any of the code, they wouldn't just cut off funds to the Pool and Eva's company, they would also sue Eva's company for damages. Eva's company had no assets except Eva herself, and she was highly valuable. The legal question of whom she belonged to was still unresolved, so any lawsuit was likely to be extremely expensive, and might end with Eva finding that she belonged to SMI, a piece of property they could do what they liked with . . .

Eva was amazed. She'd known before she got home that Mom was going to be upset—very upset—and Dad might be angry, which he had been. But this level of fuss! It was almost mad, except that Mom and Dad didn't seem quite so surprised.

"Now is this all quite clear to you too, Eva?" Ms. Callaway had said.

"On a talk show or something—if they ask me?"

"You must support the policies and products of the companies in question."

"Uh-uh."

"In that case you had better refuse invitations to appear on programs other than those in which an agreed list of questions is adhered to. This will somewhat restrict your appearances, I'm afraid."

"Okay. Provided they don't stop me from going to the Reserve."

Ms. Callaway didn't know about the Reserve and looked blank.

"If you must," said Mom.

"Out of harm's way," said Dad.

"I must further emphasize," said Ms. Callaway, "that SMI owns complete rights to all reproductions of any performance by Eva, and this includes the unfortunate episode last night. They will refuse permission for all future showings of it, and any such showings will be illegal. All tapes will be regarded as pirated, and their owners prosecuted. Any support by you for such a showing, public or private, will be treated as a breach of the contract, with the consequences I have spoken of. I expect you recorded the conference—may I have the tape, please?''

It was still in the shaper. Eva hadn't seen it—she'd been waiting for a moment when Mom wasn't around. Now Dad took it out without a word and gave it to Ms. Callaway, who put it in her briefcase and left. She hadn't said anything about Grog that time. That came later.

Eva had only begun to understand what she'd done as the day went on.

"That was something!" Cormac had exclaimed. "That was really *something*!"

"You were great!" Bren had told her.

"Terrific!" Ginny had agreed.

Mr. Sellig had wanted to scrap the prepared subject for that afternoon's ethics lesson and have a discussion on animal rights, but Eva had told him she wasn't allowed to.

On the news programs that evening rival companies had shown pictures of chimps, and extinct animals, and were snide about the fact that SMI was refusing permission to let anyone show the sequence.

Grog had called. It was difficult with Mom in the room, so Eva had answered mainly with grunts.

"How's things?"

"Mmmm."

"Lil and Dan not too happy?"

"Uh."

"Tell them I'm sorry—no, better not. From my point of view it was . . . hell, Eva, I'd never guessed—I was just keeping my fingers crossed and you came up with *that*!"

"Uh?"

"Not seen it yet?"

"Uh-uh."

"You'd better be quick. SMI is going flat out to suppress every damn tape. Anyway, it's just what I wanted. We're off. I'm setting up office tomorrow."

"Uh!"

(The idea of Grog in an office was a contradiction in terms.)

"Sure. You've opened the gates. It's a tide. It's a wave. Now we've got to ride it. See you."

He hung up.

"Grog?" Mom had asked.

"Uh."

"It's all his fault."

Three days later a letter had come from Ms. Callaway saying that any attempt on Eva's part to see or talk to Giorgio Kennedy or any persons connected with any organization set up by him for the return of chimpanzees to a natural habitat would be treated as a breach of contract.

So from then on, no Grog, no face-to-face. Eva saw him quite often on the shaper, though, leading marches, lobbying politicians, addressing meetings. The cameras wouldn't be interested in him, but he always seemed to have one of their darlings along with him, some singer, some sports star, some billionaire's boyfriend. Before long the demos were big enough to attract the shaper cameras in their own right. There were banners with slogans, and a symbol—not a chimp but a broken butterfly, one bright wing ripped apart. More and more you saw the same symbol sprayed on to walls as you were driven around the city. Kids at school started coming for autographs again, bringing cards with the broken butterfly printed in one corner.

"Uh-uh," Eva said, and explained that she wasn't allowed to, but she signed a separate piece of paper for them to stick on to the card later. Grog had been right, she realized. The movement was a wave. She could feel it all the time now, in the way people reacted to her. The singers and sports stars were only the glitter at the crest, but underneath came the growing surge of ordinary people, millions now, thinking the same thoughts, asking the same questions, moving in the same direction to the same end.

Early one evening, before Mom was home, Mimi Venturi telephoned.

"Eva, my pretty, is something I wish to discuss. I have this idea."

"Uh?"

"You come here, to my apartment? Tuesday morning."

"I thought we were doing a commercial."

"Is cancelled. That stupid Grog."

"Uh?"

"All his fault. You come?"

"You know I'm not allowed to talk to him?"

"Is in Berlin. No time for his poor Mama. That boy!"

"How is he?"

"Is well. Is happy. Is boring—I send a car."

"Okay."

Mimi's apartment was a good kilometer in the air. A real butler answered the door.

"Ms. Venturi is not yet home," he said. "If you do not mind waiting."

He showed Eva into the living room. It was almost dark, because the blinds were down, shutting out what must have been a stupendous view. Grog was sitting in an armchair reading a file.

Eva hesitated a moment, then scuttled across the carpet and leaped onto his lap. He laughed and ran his fingers across her pelt. Eagerly she began an inspection of his new beard.

"Great to see you," he said. "You don't have to worry— mother smuggled me in."

"Sh. Cormac's in the hall."

"I've told Bill to settle him down in front of a good loud space epic. How's things? Difficult at home?"

"Uh."

"Poor Lil—wish I could talk to her."

"No good."

"Not yet—someday, maybe. I've been in touch with Dan—he'll swing around."

"Huh!"

"We're going to need him. He knows a lot of essential stuff. When he finds where the future's going, he'll join. I don't mean just to stay working. He's enough of a scientist to want to be where the real stuff is happening. Now sit still. There's something I want to show you. I'm just back from a demo in Berlin—our biggest yet. I've got a tape. Look."

He switched the shaper on. The zone filled with people walking toward the camera, ten abreast. It closed in on a tiny figure in the front rank, blue-eyed, golden-haired, wearing a pair of green overalls with a broken butterfly on the bib. Eva recognized her at once—Tanya Olaf had rocketed up the charts out of nowhere five months ago and stayed at the top ever since.

"Whoo!" said Eva.

"Looks good in our get-up," said Grog.

Eva caught a glimpse of him marching in the rank behind, a little to the left. She felt a silly pang of jealousy—since she'd been stopped from going on talk shows she hadn't been meeting people like Tanya.

"What's she like?" she said.

"Pure bitch, doesn't give a damn about chimps but knows the right place to be seen. Done us a song—not bad—you'll hear it. Now that fellow there, the one with the blue chin, he's going to be useful. He's General Secretary of DKFD—that's the main European . . ."

"Whoo!"

Eva had snorted because the zone had changed. The camera had swung up and at the same time withdrawn until Tanya and Grog and the other leaders had dwindled to tiny figures at the bottom of the zone and behind them she now could see, stretching away down the tree-lined boulevard, out of sight in the distance but still coming on, thousands beyond thousands, the rest of the march.

"Good moment," said Grog.

"You got all those people out?"

"You got them out. Didn't you realize that? I've just been working on the results."

The scene jumped. It was dusk now, a different street, the march going by, singing, faces under the lamp glare, the broken butterfly everywhere. And now it was a sports arena, every seat full and a solid mass of people crammed on to the central space around a floodlit stage. The music stopped and the lights went out. Silence, and then a bay of cheering as a public zone sprang up on the stage—a table draped with blue cloth, a woman speaking into a microphone, on one side of her a gray-haired man with a fretful look and on the other, sitting up on the table in a withdrawn huddle, a chimp in yellow overalls.

There was a curious note in the cheering, not just excitement but challenge.

"First time we've risked it in public," said Grog.

"I've never seen it."

"You haven't! *They* all have."

The woman sat down. The man grabbed the microphone. The heads of journalists bobbed in the foreground. In the sudden silence you could hear their calls and the man bleating, "One at a time, please." You could feel the huge crowd holding its breath, waiting. The chimp jumped to her feet and barked. The sound was like an explosion, ringing out and then echoing off the cliffs of the arena. The cameras closed in till she filled the zone, staring at the crowd. Her rage, her misery, were solid things, as tangible and visible as the table beneath her. She paused and then, with a single firm movement, gripped the bib of her overalls in both hands, lifted the hem to her mouth, bit, and tore. The rasp of the rending cloth filled the night. The bright butterfly fell in two. With her black pelt shining under the lights as if electric with animal energies, the chimp knuckled along the table, blotting out the two humans as she passed them, and was gone.

The cheering rose, the roar of the human wave. There was a new note in it now, more than the challenge to the fat-cat companies that had been trying to suppress the tape, a sense of excitement, of something special and extraordinary having happened. Eva could feel it too, with her human mind. A message had been passed, an immense gap bridged. The movements of the chimp on the table had expressed what Eva had felt at the conference—she'd known that at the time—but she now saw that they said much more. They spoke for Kelly and the other chimps and all the children of earth, the orangs and giraffes and whales and moths and eagles, which over the past few centuries had turned their backs on humankind and crawled or glided or sunk away into the dark.

"Terrific moment," said Grog. "Time you saw it."

"Not art," said Mimi's voice from the door. "Therefore not great moment."

"Just don't talk crap, Mother," said Grog.

She sprang forward, her red cape swirling behind her, a handful of bangles swinging like brass knuckles. Eva jumped clear in time for Grog to catch the flailing arm by the wrist and pull his mother down onto his lap, where he pinioned her close. It was clearly a movement they'd had plenty of practice at.

"You say crap to your mother—you who are snatching the bread from my mouth!"

"Hey! So it's right about the bread!"

"Already I told you! The banana merchants are trying to cancel my contract! They will pay me in blood! Eva, call McAulliffe!"

"Uh?" said Eva.

"Her lawyer," said Grog. "She calls him nine times a day. Now wait a moment, Mother. I'm going to let you go, and if you bite me, Eva's going to bite you right back. Show her your teeth, Eva—give them a good gnash. Ouch! You . . . ! Get her, Eva!"

Mimi was on her feet, calmly undoing the clasp of her cloak. With a queenly gesture she flung it over Grog and turned smiling to Eva. Eva snickered back at her. She liked Mimi—Mimi would have gotten on well in the Reserve, she thought. Grog tossed the cloak aside and sat licking his forearm.

"Let's get this straight," he said. "Honeybear is definitely trying to stop the chimp commercials because our boycott is beginning to pressure them!"

"I will not pressure them only, I will massacre them! Get me McAulliffe!"

"Hold it, hold it. What are they going to do instead? Why can't they go back to the series they had you lined up for before Eva came along?"

"Because the little poof who dreamed it up has gone off to a new agency, using same idea for different yucky drink."

"So they're stuck. Great. It's a bit early, but we've got to ride the wave. We've got to have some kind of success to show our people, or the movement's going to fold. Nobody's got any staying power any longer. Okay. Mother, you really reckon you can make yourself enough of a nuisance to World Fruit for them to think it's worth buying you off?"

"You never read your old mother's contracts? Works of art! Works of art!"

"Right, you can go on massacring them till they buy you off by giving you some kind of control over the next series of chimp commercials."

"Uh!" said Eva.

"Don't worry," said Grog. "I've got it all worked out, I hope. We've got to be lucky, but if we all push in the right direction we might swing it. I'm going to offer World Fruit a deal. I can't call off the boycott—too much of a let-down—but I can tell them we'll play it down, provided they announce that when they've finished this series of commercials they will shoot a new series in a natural location, using chimps behaving the way chimps used to in the wild."

"Out of your mind, child?" said Mimi. "Me, a wildlife director? What should I *wear*?"

"Black jodhpurs, crimson trimmings? Parakeet on your shoulder?"

"Be serious."

"I *am* serious. You won't have to direct anything. What you've got to do is use any say McAulliffe can work into your contract to see that the location they actually settle for is a place called St. Hilaire."

"Uh?" said Eva.

"Island off Madagascar. Extinct volcano. Used to be solid forest till it was felled a couple of hundred years ago. Now it's bare rocks, apart from a few pockets of real old trees the loggers couldn't reach. It's no good for tourists, no beaches and hot as hell, with the odd cyclone thrown in in a bad year. And it belongs to World Fruit. There's one bit of flat land where they've got a cocoa plantation, but it's never been economically viable and now they've got a virus. The point is it's just about the only location they *can* use. There's patches of trees that are small enough to enclose. My movement can insist on a genuinely natural location and the chimps having time to get used to being there. Even World Fruit isn't going to get permission to move into somewhere like Cayamoro. What d'you think, Eva?''

Eva shrugged. It seemed so trivial, this stuff about commercials and sponsors, after what she'd just seen on the shaper. Was this all that marvelous surge of human energy, that great wave of love and hope and anger, was going to produce? What difference would it make when the filming was over? A few eased human consciences. Nothing that mattered. Eva didn't understand Grog's excitement at all. Anyway, there were all sorts of problems he didn't seem to have thought of. She started with an obvious one.

"Chimps behaving as chimps. They don't know how."

"Who don't?"

"Jenny and the others. Trained to wear clothes. Only know what it's like in the Public Section."

"So we can't take *them*—that's why we'll be taking chimps from the Reserve. Lana, Dinks, Sniff . . .''

"Whuh!"

"You'll have to pick the others. Two males besides Sniff, and that'll mean a dozen females, won't it? Youngsters and babies."

"Whuh?"

"You're not going to St. Hilaire just to shoot a few commercials. You don't imagine that's all I've been sweating my guts for or why I got you along here now? Listen . . .''

Eva listened. Her pelt stirred. Her human mind kept telling her it could never work, never even begin, but while Grog talked her body became restless with excitement and she prowled the rich room, imagining shadows, imagining odors, imagining trees.

YEAR TWO, MONTH TWELVE, DAYS TWO AND THREE

Living in a new world . . .
Heavy, vegetable odors . . .
Racket of insects, clatter of birds . . .
Heat . . .

Dopey still with drugs the chimps stared at the daylight. They felt the steamy heat, breathed the strange air. Their yesterday —nearly three days ago, in fact—had been spent huddled into the caves of the Reserve, with wind-whipped snow scurrying around the concrete outside. They had slept through the flights and stopovers. Only Eva—awake for the journey—had seen the various changes until the final airboat had slanted out of tropic blaze into a ridged mass of cloud, felt its way down through the murk and emerged over a huge dark sea. She had not seen the island until they circled to land, but then there it was. She had pressed her muzzle to the window, misting the glass with her breath. At first what she saw didn't make sense, but then she had realized that what she was look-ing at was mainly a mountain rising almost directly from the sea, with its top all fuzzed out by the cloud base. Below that, desolation, vast jumbled slopes of bare brownish storm-eroded rock. Only here and there, darker streaks and patches, the fragmentary remains of what had once been forest before the trees had been stripped away for timber or firewood, or simply for a patch of fresh earth somebody hoped to raise a couple of crops from before the summer rains washed it away; but in these few places, in ravines and on slopes too steep to reach, the last trees still stood.

The flight path curved on. A flatter, greener area appeared. The sea came nearer, slow ocean rollers freckled with foam. Surf along rocky shores, buildings around a small harbor, trees in patterned rows, touchdown.

That had been Eva's yesterday. She could have slept in a bed but chose to spend the night with the still-doped chimps so that she would wake among them, be already one of them as they first moved out into this other world. She had awakened before any of the others, and seen Colin bending over Lana, taking her pulse, lifting an eyelid.

"Uh?"

"Morning, Eva. Stopped raining, you'll be glad to know. Does that every day, apparently, this time of year, unless there's a storm. Comes on drenching at four, thirty millimeters of rain in three hours, and that's it."

"Uh?" said Eva again, pointing at Lana.

"Not long now. That little guy's stirring, look, and there's a big fellow pretty well awake next door. They'll all be whooping about outside by lunchtime. I'm looking forward to this—it's really something."

Eva had grunted agreement. The same excitement ran through the whole team. They all felt themselves to be doing something extraordinary, even though it was only three weeks (they thought) and then back to the city, to winter, and the chimps huddling again in the caves of the grim Reserve. But for the moment it was as though they felt they were in at the birth of a new world, with the old tired world waiting and watching. Even the cameramen, who had seen so much they never admitted they were impressed by anything, couldn't quite hide their excitement.

But in Eva's case there was more than excitement—there was fear too, dry mouth, crawling pelt, drumming heart, cold weight in the stomach. She wasn't planning to make her move for at least ten days, but the thought and the fear were there. She watched Wang finger sleepily at Lana's side. Dinks's two-month-old Tod, was stirring too—the vets had had to give the babies smaller and more frequent shots, so they woke more readily. Colin left. Eva followed him out and was watching him lower the door of the next crate when she heard a quiet snort close behind her. She spun round and saw Sniff's face peering through the door of the crate Colin had already visited. She knuckled over, crouched, and greeted him. There was no Tatters here, no Geronimo. Sniff would have to settle with Billy and Herman who was boss. They were older and stronger. It was important to build up his confidence.

He acknowledged her greeting with a grunt but continued to stare out at the scene beyond. She settled beside him in the doorway, looking at it too, seeing it now as far as she could with his eyes, this totally strange place, nothing like anything he'd known.

What did he see? A patch of reddish jumbled scree sloping down toward him—nothing square, nothing flat, nothing he was used to. Beyond that, dusty green hummocks—bushes—on one side. Denser green—thick growth around a scurry of water. Red scree sloping sharply up on the left. Beyond all that, much taller green, dark shadows—trees. Buzz of insects, reek of tropic growth, steamy air under low sky. A bird, bright yellow, dipping across, calling wheep-wheep-wheep. Sniff was shivering with excitement and alarm. Eva groomed for several minutes along the twitching surface of his upper arm, then rose, knuckled a few paces forward, turned, and held out her hand, palm up. Come.

He stared, snorted more loudly, took the first pace and halted, his eyes flickering from side to side.

Come.

This time he grunted and followed her up beside the

stream, into the shadows. Behind them the hidden cameras watched them go. It was about twenty minutes before they returned to wait for the others to wake, to take them out, and show them what they had discovered.

The advance team had found the place, about three hectares of real forest they could actually reach. The rains that had stripped the mountain bald had washed most of the earth out into the sea, but here and there the shape of the underlying rock had trapped pockets of soil on which fresh growth could begin. The lower end of this patch was a steep-sided valley, thick with shrubs and saplings. Farther up it closed to a sheer-walled ravine, beyond human reach, where older trees still rooted deep into the rock. Out of sight over the bare ridges on either side ran a tall electric fence. The humans camped in the dying cocoa groves well over a kilometer below.

There were remote-controlled cameras hidden throughout the area. The idea was that everything the chimps did would be filmed, with Eva helping by seeing they were often in camera range and also by setting up events and interactions to stimulate them. SMI would edit the film for wild-life programs, and suitable sections would also be dubbed with sophisticated human voices and used for commercials for Honeybear. There ought to be enough in the can after three weeks' filming for everyone to go home. It was silly, trivial, a total waste of time and money, but none of that mattered.

It had looked as if it were going to matter at first. When they'd found out what it was going to cost, the accountants had tried to object, but by then the news had gotten out (Grog's friends had seen to that) that World Fruit was planning to take twenty chimps to a natural habitat for an experimental period, and see what happened. The bare rumor had done more for their sales than a whole season of commercials. From being world villains they found themselves world heroes. The expedition was news. By nightfall billions of eyes would have seen that first shot, the dark shapes of two chimpanzees knuckling in silence away into the trees.

Lana was awake, inspecting Wang. Abel was already at the door, peering out bright-eyed, too young to be frightened. Dinks was stirring. The stale reek of the crate was horrible after the live air. Eva beckoned from the door to Lana, who huddled back against the crate wall. She beckoned again. Then behind her a new noise started, a loud repeated hoot as Sniff stamped to and fro in front of the four crates, threshing the ground with a branch he had broken from a bush. The familiar sound seemed to encourage Lana, who came to the door and peered out. Eva put her arm around her and kissed her, encouraging her, telling her this was a good place. There were faces at the other doors now, and the sight of one another, and of Sniff displaying to and fro, seemed to give the chimps heart. Several came out into the open, sniffing and staring around. Eva could feel their wonder, their excitement and nerves. It was all so strange, so unprepared-for. And yet, and yet . . . How many of them, besides herself, had dreamed the dream? Surely she couldn't be the only one.

Suddenly a half-grown male called Berry broke from the trance. He rushed up the slope, tore a branch from the nearest bush and rushed to and fro, beating the branch around and hooting, half in imitation of what Sniff had been doing and half in sheer excitement and joy. The others watched him for a moment and then began to move too. They gathered at the edge of the stream and stared amazed at the rushing water. Eva joined them and crouched down to drink. The water had a sweetish, mineral taste, quite different from the many-times-treated water in the troughs of the Reserve. Perhaps the drugs made you thirsty, because almost at once the rest of the group was doing the same. When Eva rose and turned she saw Sniff and Herman sitting side by side, chewing steadily at some leaves they had torn from a bush.

There had been a lot of discussion back home about whether and how to feed the chimps during the experiment. Botanists on the preliminary expedition to the island had reported that there was enough food in the ringed patch to support twenty chimps for three weeks, provided they knew what to look for. Probably only some of the leaves were edible, and one particular bush was fairly poisonous but tasted so bitter that you knew at once and spat it out. (Eva had tested some of the samples the botanists had brought home.) There were wild fig trees, and mangoes that must have seeded from crop trees planted by people before the mountains went bald. There were roots too, probably, if you knew what to look for, and ant's nests and grubs under the bark of old trees up the ravine. Three hectares wasn't a lot for twenty chimps—it would be looking fairly bashed around by the time they left. Eva had been especially interested in everything the botanists could tell her. It was going to be more important than people knew. But for the moment she was thankful that Dad and the others had decided they would have to come in at night while the chimps were sleeping and leave extra food around.

She knuckled over to Herman and put her muzzle close to the fist that clasped the leaves. He cuffed her casually away— he was a big young male, strong and not very intelligent, but placid and with less than the usual share of male chimp mischief. Sniff had seen the exchange. He snapped a few twigs from the bush and passed them to Eva, who took them and munched experimentally. The taste was faintly nutty, and all but the young leaves at the tips took a lot of chewing. Not many vitamins there, she guessed. Not much else either. Chimps in the wild, Dad said, used to spend two-thirds of their day looking for food and the rest eating it when they'd found it.

By now the rest of the group had gathered around and was snatching twigs from the tree and trying the bushes nearby. Billy found a bitter one and spat the leaves out with a grunt of disgust, then went and washed his mouth out in the stream. They were used to being fed in their caves soon after they awoke, so they kept making trips back to the crates to see whether breakfast had come yet. Eva was hungry too but waited. She felt it was important not to always be the one who did things first.

In the end it was Sniff. He took Herman by the wrist and led him to the gap in the bushes he and Eva had found earlier. At the opening he turned and beckoned to Eva. Come. She rose and signaled to Lana and Dinks, but it was Abel, who nowadays associated Eva in his mind with amusements and games, who came scampering across. Beth followed, tut-tutting, so Lana picked up Wang and came too. Eva turned and led them into the shadows, aware by the sounds behind her that the rest of the group would trail along.

By midmorning they were up in the ravine. They had found figs and a trailing plant with sweet yellow berries and some slow white grubs in a mound of dead leaves—they tasted like shrimp without the sea flavor—and a bog plant with long pale leaves whose midrib you could crunch like celery. They had also begun to learn that trees were not as easy to climb as they looked, especially if you were used to the rigid steel branches welded to the pillars of the Reserve. Herman had one crashing fall into the bushes below and rose bewildered, still clutching the branch that had snapped on him. By now they'd eaten enough for the moment, and it was getting too hot to move, so they rested.

There were two trees of the same kind, with smooth gray many-forked branches, growing low down from opposite cliffs of the ravine and meeting over the rush of water. Two hidden cameras up in the cliffs were trained on the place, but Eva

hadn't needed to coax the others there. They had found it of
their own accord and swung themselves up, draping their bodies into crooks and crotches, making a pattern of dark strong
shapes against the snaking gray branches. They twitched or
scratched or groomed for a while at a neighbor, or moved
lethargically to a fresh perch or to join another chimp, but for
the most part they stayed still.

Eva sat at the edge of the group and watched them. Deliberately she lived in the moment, refusing to think about what
lay ahead. She could not imagine that she would ever be so
happy again, so filled with tingling, sparkling peace. Of course
it was too hot for scampering around, though the spray from
the stream helped, but she could feel that there was more to
the stillness of the chimps than that. It was something shared,
like a song, the wonder, the amazement, the deep content, the
sense of having come home. She did not have to guess but
knew, because she could feel the awareness going to and fro
among them, shared and real, that they understood what had
happened. The part that mattered, anyway. All of them, wide
awake, were remembering and recognizing the dream. If nothing else happened, or if everything she and Grog had planned
went wrong, this hour, this noon, would have been worth-
while.

In the early afternoon Eva experimented with making herself a nest. She was going to have to teach the others, so it was
important to get it right herself first. It was easy, once you'd
learned to recognize the sort of branches needed, close and
whippy enough to bend and then lace together, holding them
in place with your weight. Later still, she seemingly accidentally coaxed the chimps up the southern slope outside the
ravine to where the humans had left the day's rations—
mostly plain chimp chow, with enough bananas to go around.
Sniff and Billy had their first set-to, not a proper fight, but
bluffing and challenging, and then, before anything serious

happened, settling down to intense close mutual grooming.
They were still at it when the rain started.

It came almost in an instant, a few large drops rattling
among the leaves and then a drenching downpour. Everything
streamed wet. Twenty dark faces—twenty-one including
Tod's—stared disgusted at the sky, and then the whole group
went knuckling rapidly from the hill for the cover of their
crates. The crates were gone. Eva had known they would be
and had heard earlier that afternoon the thud of rotor blades
as a flivver lifted them away. The chimps halted and stared at
the blank space in dismay. The stream was roaring now with a
dangerous sound, which added to their alarm. Across the valley, below where the crates had been, stretched the electric
fence.

The fence had become the biggest problem in the whole
expedition. The sponsors nearly called it off because of the
cost and difficulty, but everyone had agreed that without one
the chimps would probably go roving across the barren mountain to other patches of forest, almost impossible for humans
to reach, and be lost completely. Even as it was, the whole
program was months late, because the fence had taken so long
to build. There should have been sun and sparkling waters,
instead of this daylong sauna.

Now the chimps gazed at the fence and the barren slope
beyond. To their minds there was no other place the crates
could have gone but down there. Several of them knuckled
over to the fence to look, naturally enough reaching hands to
grip the mesh as they did so. They leaped back with barks of
dismay, then gingerly reached forward and tried again, snatching their hands back at the first tingle. Some of them perhaps
knew about electric fences, because there were places around
the Reserve where possible escape routes had been blocked
with charged wire, but they wouldn't all have explored that
far.

The rain, if anything, was heavier now. For a few minutes they scuttered to and fro along the fence, as if hoping for a gap. Sniff, more purposefully, traced the line up the right-hand ridge and over to where it turned and climbed toward the cloud base. He paused at the angle, staring out over the barren, horrible rockscape, all streaming with thousands of individual tiny waterfalls, then snorted and turned away. Eva had followed, interested both in the fence and in Sniff's reactions, and when he saw her he snorted on a slightly different, negative, note, and led the way back down into the valley. The others were already heading up into the comparative shelter of the trees.

In the ravine the stream was a foaming fawn torrent, but near its lower end rose a stand of broad-leaved palms, with dryish patches beneath them. Here they huddled together, their drenched pelts steaming. Night fell, and suddenly they were in total dark. By the time the rain stopped an hour later, they were all asleep, but Eva, restless, awoke and saw lights moving around. Her first thought was that Dad or some of his helpers had come up to check that they were all right, but then she realized that the lights were too faint and there were far too many of them, hundreds, thousands, blinking their different codes. Fireflies. Of course. She lay for a while, listening to the roar of the stream, and at last fell truly asleep.

Sniff explored the fence in the morning. Eva had expected him to, just as he seemed to have expected her to come around with him. It was another steamy hot day, but the cloud base was higher so that you could see most of the way up the mountain. Even for chimps the climb was stiff going—for the humans who had built the fence it must have been quite a task. Every so often Sniff would stop and gingerly touch the mesh, to check that the current was active all along. At other times he paused and simply stared at the mountainside, all brownish dull rock and scree, glaring with the heavy diffused light, plunging toward the sea. From up here you could see the grove spreading across the cramped plain at the foot of the mountain, the regular green rows mottled brown with disease.

During one of his pauses Sniff gazed at the area with deep interest, then grunted, nudged Eva and pointed, not at the grove but out beyond to the tip of the island, the little harbor with a ship loading, and in an open patch beside the buildings the SMI airboat tethered firm and the two flivvers, tiny as toys with distance. His snort expressed wariness and distrust.

The fence turned again, running sideways across the slope now and climbed steeply to cross the ridge that lower down became the left-hand flank of their valley. At the crest Sniff halted. This was the highest point of the enclosure. From here you could see a whole new expanse of mountain, almost the same as the other side but steeper, with sheer cliff in places and in others loose rock at such a slope that it seemed poised for a fresh fall. There was another difference. About two kilometers away, nearer to the peak, was a large patch of dull green—trees.

They were too far off for Eva to tell whether they were real trees, or just bushes that had somehow retained their roothold on the incredible slope, but she could understand why they'd never been cleared—there was almost no way any human could reach them. She stared and stared. It was no use trying to work out a possible route—too much of the slope between was hidden—but she couldn't help trying. "Take as many of the others as you can with you," Grog had said. "If the worst comes to the worst you'll have to go alone. Give me a month." Grog had never been on the island—he'd only seen photographs. From them it looked as if there'd be places to hide and enough to eat. He couldn't have known.

She heard Sniff grunt and turned. He was already climbing

back down the ridge toward the ravine. Eva waited. She heard him crashing about below, and then he came back carrying a small branch he had torn from a bush. When he reached the fence he put the branch against it, at first just brushing the leaf tips quickly along and then withdrawing it. Feeling no shock, he pushed harder. The mesh bowed out under his weight, but the fence had been engineered to stand such attacks—Dad would know that the chimps were smart enough to try something like that if they chose—and the branch broke first.

Sniff wasn't ready. He fell solidly against the wire and got the full force of the current. All his hair shot erect. He jumped back and might have gone tumbling helplessly down toward the stream if Eva hadn't grabbed at his arm and caught him. He didn't seem to know what he was doing. She eased him into a crouch, where he stayed gasping while she tried to calm him by grooming the trembling pelt along his spine. At last he gave a long sigh and straightened, then turned his head to gaze at the trees on the far slope. He got up, went back to the fence, and studied it minutely, his muzzle only a few inches away from the mesh. After a while, with a grunt of disappointment he continued their exploration down the slope but now didn't pause either to test the current or to look at the mountain.

Just as they were gathering for their midday rest in the ravine, a whooping noise began from down the slope. It was, in fact, the recorded call of a howler monkey, chosen because it was natural enough not to alarm the chimps but couldn't be mistaken for anything else. If it had come in short bursts, it would have been a signal that Dad or someone wanted to see her urgently, but the steady unbroken version just meant Come if you can. Sniff had come back from his reconnoiter in an aggressive mood and had had several confrontations with Billy. Now they were making it up, clasped together, absorbedly peering and combing each other's fur. Nobody but Sniff would have been likely to keep an eye on Eva. Slowly she edged herself clear and slipped away.

Dad was waiting by the gate, fanning the flies away with a branch. Sweat streamed down his beard.

"Having fun?" he said.

Eva grunted enthusiasm.

"And your pals?"

"Uh."

"The shaper chaps are pleased with the pictures they're getting. There's one long sequence, yesterday, when you were settling into those trees in the gorge. That was lovely to see. Like a Japanese print."

He had brought the keyboard. Eva picked it up and pressed the keys.

"Lovely to do," she said.

Eva had heard the enthusiasm in his voice and was glad but at the same time bothered. In a few days' time she was going to let him down very badly. He was doing his best for her and for the chimps, he thought. He really wanted them to be happy. He loved them, in his way. Probably he understood them better than any human alive, but still she didn't dare tell him.

"What happened up at the top of the enclosure this morning?" he said.

"Uh?"

"We saw you and Sniff going off on your fence survey. Characteristic—he's a very bright lad. We don't have any cameras right up there in the open, so the next thing we knew was the alarm bell ringing in the camp. The circuit didn't break, so we left it until we saw you coming back down the far side."

Inwardly Eva frowned. They hadn't told her about the alarm bell.

"He fell against the fence," she said. "He'd been testing it with a branch. He's learned now."

"You don't think we ought to get cameras up there?"

"He was just looking. He's like that. They won't run off. They're happy here."

"That's my line. I must say, I'll be sorry for them when we've got to go."

"Me too. Heard from Mom?"

"I'll be calling her tonight."

"Give her my love."

"Of course."

Eva handed him the keyboard and knuckled back up to the ravine. The moment she appeared Sniff swung across through the branches and faced her, bristling. When she crouched and panted he came close and smelled her all over, then faced her again, less challengingly but with a look of querying suspicion. She reached up and stroked his cheek before offering him her shoulder to groom. He grunted softly and began, while Eva sat hunched and thinking.

The alarm bell was a problem. On the other hand it was good to know for sure that there were no cameras up at the top. She'd been told about the cameras in the valley, because of being expected to maneuver the chimps in front of them, so she ought to be able to construct a mental map of the areas that weren't in range. In one of those areas she'd have to find and break off a long straight branch, preferably with a fork at the end and strong enough to bear Sniff's weight. Then, still keeping out of range, she'd have to take it up and stow it somewhere near the top.

Food? It might be possible to hoard some chimp chow. They'd found enough food in the trees yesterday not to eat all their ration last night. There were no cameras trained on the feeding area, because the whole idea was to show the chimps living wild. Chimp chow would be a let-down. But how to store it and carry enough to see four or five chimps through the first day or so . . .

Four or five? Well, Sniff would come. Eva was as sure of that as if he'd told her in words. Lana was no adventurer, but she'd have to be made to, somehow. Two more at the most. Who? How?

And when? The obvious time for a breakout was early dawn. With a little luck it would be hours before the watchers below were sure enough in their counting to know you were missing, but you'd never get chimps to behave like that. Chimps liked to wake slowly and sit around and scratch and groom one another, reminding themselves who and where they were and how they fitted into the group. They'd never be restless enough for action till at least midmorning, and by then the humans below would be watching . . .

And now the alarm bell . . .

Eva heard a gloomy, meditative grunt and realized that she had made it herself. Sniff stopped grooming. He put his hand to her face and turned her head so that he could stare into her eyes. His gaze was clear, deep, and steady. After a while he grunted, using almost exactly the same tone that she had. What was he thinking? Could he actually read her thoughts? There was something shared anyway, she was certain, not the detailed plans, but at least the idea of escape and the feelings that went with it. Difficult. Frightening. Necessary.

YEAR TWO,
MONTH TWELVE,
DAY TEN

Living in tension, waiting . . .
Waking—will the chance come today?
Noon, heat, peace in the ravine, the humans below all
  resting —now?
Not yet.
Dusk, with drenching rain, tree smell and sea smell.
  Tomorrow . . . ?
Perhaps.

Eva heard the howler while she was still trying to settle herself into her pelt for the day, fingering around, nosing and
nibbling under the hairs, the way you did. She was conscious
of having slept badly, for once, and now her fur didn't seem to
want to lie down. The others were uneasy too. She could
sense a restlessness, a nerviness. They kept glancing up between the leaves, where the clouds moved low and dark and
faster than usual. Then she heard the signal, a burst, cut
short, and another burst, and a gap, and again . . . urgent.

Lana was giving Wang his morning once-over. Sniff was
grooming Herman—he'd had a run-in with Billy yesterday
that had ended with Billy chasing him up a tree, so now he'd
evidently decided to make a serious alliance with the much
less ambitious third male. The others were fidgety, preoccupied. It was no problem to slip away.

She found Dad inside the fence, with the expedition coordi-
nator, Maria, and Diego, who'd headed the advance party and
built the enclosure. They were all three looking at the sky.

Out here you could really see how low and dark the clouds were and how fast they were traveling. The wind was up too—she hadn't heard it in the ravine because of the noise of the stream. It was like no wind Eva had ever felt, a huge block of steamy heat moving all together, like the breath out of a mile-wide mouth.

"We've got trouble," said Dad. "There's a typhoon on the way. It was supposed to pass on the other side of Madagascar, but now it's swung in."

"I told 'em," said Diego.

"Uh?"

"Apparently we've got about five hours. It's too late to evacuate. Maria wants to get the chimps in."

"I'm getting the crates lifted up," said Maria. "If you can get the chimps down here, we'll put some doped fruit out."

"Uh-uh," said Eva and took the keyboard from Dad.

"Don't think I can," she explained. "I'm not boss. Sniff's having trouble with Billy."

"Good grief," said Maria. "Couldn't we lay a trail of fruit?"

"I doubt if you'd get them all," said Dad.

"What are you going to do with them?" said Eva. "When you've got them?"

"Keep them in the crates till it's over," said Dad in a flat tone. Knowing him so well, Eva could tell that this was all part of an argument that he'd lost.

"Uh-uh."

"It's the best we can do," said Maria.

"Spoil everything," said Eva.

"It's not just that," said Dad. "Just think what it would be like in the crates, with a typhoon going on. It wouldn't necessarily be any safer, in my opinion."

"I told 'em, I told 'em," said Diego.

"It was getting that damn fence built," said Maria. "Listen,

Eva, you realize there's every chance that ravine will fill with water, and you'll all be drowned."

"Uh?" said Eva, looking at Dad. He shrugged.

"Can't tell," said Diego. "Must've been typhoons before. The trees in there have stood it."

"We can climb out, up," said Eva. "Blossom found a way."

"Yes, we saw that," said Dad.

"Why does something like this *always* have to happen?" said Maria. "Every damn project I've ever been on. The better it's going, the worse it comes."

"You might get some terrific pictures," said Eva.

She said it on purpose. At first she'd just been reacting to the immediate problem, the typhoon, and whether she could get the others down and what was the best thing to do. But from what Dad had said about the crates not being any safer she'd realized that the human argument wasn't really over, and the more weight she could put on his side the more chance there was of staying. He was right anyway. Now that she'd had time to think she was determined not to do what Maria said. If worst came to worst, she'd simply disobey orders. It wasn't that she'd planned the escape completely yet or was sure it would work or that she'd get anyone except Sniff to go with her, but a break like this . . . they'd have to keep the chimps drugged while the typhoon lasted, or they'd go mad in the crates. They might even decide they'd gotten enough film already and could all go home . . .

Maria was talking into a commo. Diego was watching the sky. All three humans were streaming with sweat.

"Well done," muttered Dad.

"How soon can you get them down here, Eva?" said Maria.

Eva shrugged. If she'd really wanted to and had enough bananas for bait, she thought she might have managed by late morning. She held up three fingers.

"Three's the best she can do," said Maria into the commo. She listened.

"Too late," she said. "They want to have the flivvers lashed down before then."

"Tell them to send up more chimp chow," said Dad. "Several days' rations. In a steel box with a lock. I'll leave the key under that rock, darling."

"What about the fence?" said Maria.

"Still have to switch the alarm off," said Diego. "That amount of wind, it'll keep setting itself off. There'll still be the current, unless we get a lightning strike. They'll lay low, won't they? None of 'em have been near the fence for days."

"What d'you think, darling?" said Dad.

"Uh?"

It took Eva a moment to gather her wits. The whole problem of crossing the fence without setting off the alarm had filled her waking mind for days. Even when she was dreaming the dream she kept finding her path between the branches blocked by live mesh.

"They wouldn't anyway," she said. "Happy where they are."

"God, if I'd been given a whole day's warning," said Maria.

"It'll be all right, my dear," said Dad. "Personally I think the chimps will be safer up here than we will down on the shoreline. The ravine is good shelter, provided the water doesn't rise too far, and as Eva says, if worst comes to worst they can always climb out."

"Least they won't have tidal waves to look out for," said Diego.

"I suppose there's that," said Maria. "Okay. You win."

"We'll be okay," said Eva.

"Let's hope," said Maria. "You'll be on your own."

* * *

The wind rose unsteadily. At full force you could hear its shriek even above the rush of the stream. In the lower part of the valley the bushes threshed like waves. And then there would be a lull, though the clouds still raced over, lower than ever now. In these pauses Eva's pelt seemed to crawl with electricity. The others presumably felt the same. They were uneasy, making short expeditions to the nearer feeding trees and heading back for the ravine after a few mouthfuls. Sniff and Billy seemed to have forgotten their conflict for the moment. Sniff in particular was anxious and now kept his eyes on Eva most of the time, and followed her around. In one of the lulls she took the chance to lead him, by a route she had worked out to avoid the cameras, up the left flank of the valley to where she had been trying during the last few days to weaken the branch she wanted by gnawing a ring around its base. He studied the bite marks, frowning, and smelled them too, then looked in a puzzled way along the length of the branch. Eva made the "Come" signal and led the way on, threading through the scrub-covered slope above where it dropped to the ravine and up on to the bare ridge at the top of the valley, close to the place where Sniff had had his shock. Here the fence crossed the ridge and immediately turned down the mountain. There was a point where you could stand on the outer slope, level with the top of the fence and only about four meters from it. A branch placed here, with its fork weighted with rocks for stability and its butt across the top of the fence . . .

Eva pointed to the place and made gestures. Sniff considered the problem, frowning. She could sense him trying to estimate distances. He grunted doubtfully, then raised his head and stared at the far trees. The upper end of the wooded patch was hidden in the cloud base. He was still looking when the lull ended. The hot wind came booming off the ocean, so strong now that they had to crouch beneath its weight. When Sniff faced it, it sleeked his pelt like silk, but when he turned for the shelter of the valley the wind got under the fur and bushed it out as if he'd been displaying. He led the way now, following the route they'd taken, down to the tree with the weakened branch. The wind was roaring through the treetops, making them bow all one way, like weeds in a stream. Sniff looked at the branch for a few seconds and began to climb. He clambered slantwise up it and gripped another, stouter branch that crossed it about five metres up. With his feet on the lower branch he heaved them apart until he was standing like a triumphant weight lifter with his arms raised above his head. The branch creaked. Eva gnawed at the straining fibers, feeling them snap as the cut opened. The branch gave with a crash, leaving Sniff dangling in midair, but he swung himself up and climbed down, panting not with the effort but with excitement. Together they twisted the branch free and broke off the twigs and side shoots. Eva wondered whether the microphones had picked up the noise. She guessed so, but the wind would cover most of it, and in any case, the chimps did a fair amount of crashing around in the ordinary course of things.

They dragged the branch up the slope and out into the open. The wind was really howling now. A human could hardly have stood in it. Sniff immediately tried to raise the branch toward the top of the fence but Eva only pretended to help. It was too soon to get that far. Diego might not have switched the alarm off yet, and in any case, suppose they did get it in place, Sniff would insist on trying to cross and then perhaps get stuck outside. But he was raring to go and almost managed it on his own before a sudden new blast of wind made him give up. Crouching under its force he glared at the fence top and the mountain beyond, then snorted and led the way back.

The others were all in the ravine, huddled together, nervous, waiting. Down here you could hardly feel the wind, but you could hear its shriek and see the black ominous clouds racing above the threshing treetops. The chimps' alarm was like an odor, something they all breathed and shared. Wang clung close to Lana, as if he'd been a baby, and Tod huddled in Dinks's arms with a wide, terrified grin. The same white fear signal gleamed on every dark face. Eva was grooming Lana, trying to calm her, when the rain started.

It struck the mountain like a flail. You heard the crash of its coming, and then you were under water. Not just drenched, drowning. Can't breathe! Tidal wave! No, of course not, not this high, but for a minute it felt like that, as though the whole ocean had hummocked itself up and crashed down on the island. Eva gasped, struggling for breath, clutching the branch beside her, forgetting everything except her own immediate survival. Below her she saw the stream leap in its bed. One moment it had been tumbling down its rocky channel in the floor of the ravine and the next it was crashing, white, from cliff to cliff. As the first wall of rain passed by, somebody scrambled, snorting, up beside her—Sweetie-pie, drenched and grinning with terror. The opposite tree had one comfortable branch that hung low, only a meter or so above the floor of the ravine. Last time Eva had looked a couple of chimps had been sitting there, but now the branch was straining in the torrent and they were gone. She peered through the downpour and saw movement, several chimps climbing higher, others reaching down to help them. Something about their attitudes, the way they had gathered on the branches closest to the cliff, told her that they were in shelter—yes, of course, when she'd been out in the open with Sniff the wind had been from that side. Carefully she made her way across the network of branches and found she was right. It was like coming into a house out of the rain, so sudden was the difference.

She went back and with some difficulty coaxed Lana to cross, and then Sweetie-pie. Seeing them go, the rest came too.

There were barely enough perches to go around. Once they were settled Eva worked her way along the huddled line and counted. Eighteen, nineteen, twenty, twenty-one. All safe. But now she couldn't find anywhere to perch herself till Sniff shoved Herman over enough on the branch they were sharing to make room for her. She settled and looked at the torrent, trying to see if it was still rising. After that first tremendous buffet of water the downpour had lessened, though it was still heavier than any rain Eva had ever seen, lashed by the wind against the farther cliff as if sprayed from firehoses. The whole mountainside must be streaming. If enough of it gathered here the ravine, as Maria had said, would fill right up, or far enough at least to tear the trees from their roothold in the cliffs. Before that happened they must move. The others, even Sniff, would be difficult to persuade, to make understand the danger. She set herself marks on the opposite cliff and tried to estimate whether the tumbling water was getting nearer. After a long while she decided it was, but slowly. No need to worry yet.

By then Eva had realized how cold it had gotten. At first her slight sense of chill seemed the natural result of drying out after her drenching, but even when she was dry she found she was shivering, and was glad of the warmth of Sniff's body. Not that it could have been cold by the standards of winter in the Reserve, but compared with the steady, steamy heat of the last week, when even chimps, who had evolved for a climate like that, had needed to rest through the middle of the day, the change was extraordinary.

How long did typhoons last? Two or three days, she seemed to remember. They were huge, intense eddies in the atmosphere, sweeping along on curving paths, weren't they? If that was right you'd get the wind blowing harder and harder the nearer the center came, with the isobars packing in, and then it would change direction—you'd only get a lull if the center passed straight over you—and you'd have about the same amount of time before it was over. Anyway, it was going to get worse before it got better. The leaves of the tree they perched in were leathery and bitter. They had already stripped the ravine of anything edible.

Time was impossible to estimate. The howling minutes seemed like hours, but Eva noticed that as the wind rose the rain seemed to get less. Night would come with its usual rush, and then it would be pitch-dark, not even a firefly for guidance. Better go now. With a grunt of decision Eva started to move through the branches, then turned and made the "Come" sign to Sniff. He looked at her as if she were mad but stayed where he was, and she went on alone.

There was no way out along the flooded floor, so she took the route Blossom had found up the farther cliff. As she came out of the shelter the wind seemed to lift her the last stretch and then try and blow her on up the slope above. Keeping low to the ground, clutching at bushes and boulders, she worked her way sideways along the slope and down into the valley.

Here the wind was less, no more than gale force, but above her it crashed through the straining treetops, making sharp explosions like gunfire where some big wet leaf was slapping itself to tatters, and shrieking between the thinner branches so loudly that Eva was forced to stop and stuff moss into her ears to try and dull the pain. The whole floor of the valley, including the patch under the palms where they usually slept, was flooded. She made her way around the edge of the water, down through the area of scrub and out into the open. The stream had gathered itself into a torrent again and was foaming down the mountain. The rain was almost over. She could see right down to the coast, and beyond that white foam and black water under a sky as dark as nightfall. Creeping close above the ground, clutching at boulders, she made her way to the place Dad had shown her, found the key, and opened the steel chest. The chimp chow came in five-kilo sacks. She took two out of the chest and relocked it, then struggled back with one bag gripped between her teeth and the other under her arm. She had to leave the second one out above the ravine in order to climb down.

In the shelter of the cliff she worked along the line of chimps, distributing the chow by handfuls. They received it without any sign of surprise or gratitude and chewed away. They were calmer now, having realized that they were safer here than they would be anywhere else. Only Wang still kept his grin of terror.

Night came with just enough warning for Eva to move out and find herself a crotch to sleep in among the more exposed branches. With difficulty she persuaded Lana to do the same, and seeing what they were up to several of the others copied them. The rain came erratically now in rattling spasms, but a few drenchings were clearly better than dropping asleep and letting go of one's hold.

Night seemed endless, cold, the snatched intervals of dozing full of roaring dreams and the terror of falling, but she must have slept at last because she was awakened by a sudden new loud noise and opened her eyes in daylight to find Sweetie-pie crouching beside her, solicitously picking the moss out of her left ear.

There were twenty-one chimps still in the tree. No one had fallen. By now they took it for granted that Eva would bring them chow. Only Sniff was interested enough to follow her up the cliff for the second bag. The wind was wilder still, coming in heavy buffeting lumps. It was blowing half sideways along the slope now, so that Eva had to work her way directly across its path to where she'd left the bag pinned down by a rock. It was only a few meters, but she barely made it. Clearly there was no hope of getting down to the chest for more until the wind dropped. There was also no hope of persuading hungry chimps to let her preserve half a bag till the evening—in fact, they were now confident enough of their safety to come crowding around when she brought the chow down and have characteristic chimp squabbles over their rations. Well, one evening without supper wouldn't kill them.

By late that morning the wind had gone around enough to blow directly up the ravine. For almost an hour it roared full force between the cliffs, while the chimps clung with all their strength to the swaying branches, grinning their fright. At one point Eva remembered the cameras. Terrific pictures, she thought. Huh.

The wind swung on. They moved to the shelter of the farther cliff and endured. Tomorrow, Eva thought. If it goes the same speed that it came. In the afternoon, when it's dying. Before the humans switch the alarm on again.

They spent the night hungry and cold. For several hours around dawn it rained, not quite as heavily as at the onset, but enough to wake the torrent below to another bout of white roaring.

As soon as the rain lessened Eva made the "Come" signal to Sniff. This time he followed. Quite a lot of trees were down, including one of the shelter palms. She unlocked the chest, bit a bag open, and let Sniff feed. She ate too. Then she gave him a fresh bag to carry and took one herself. At the top of the cliff she pinned one bag down and with some difficulty persuaded Sniff not to climb down into the ravine with the other, but to follow her on up to the top of the enclosure. The wind had picked their branch up and blown it against the fence—without that, it would have gone right out to sea. They dragged it back, and, with Eva now helping her best and the wind behind them, dropped it without trouble across the top of the fence. Sniff watched frowning while Eva pinned the fork firm with several boulders, with the bag of chow beside it.

The branch bowed deeply when Sniff put his weight on it, but stayed in place and straightened as he walked four-footed to its stiffer end. He reached the top of the fence and paused, studying the drop. The wind screamed past, rumpling his pelt. Eva barked anxiously. She'd known she'd have to take the risk of letting him get this far. Sniff glanced around. She looked up at the racing sky, turned, moved up the slope, looked at the sky again, and made the "Come" signal. He snorted and studied the drop again. For a moment she thought he would insist on going now, but a sudden stronger gust changed his mind and he made his way back, almost unbalancing as he turned. On the way to the ravine he paused several times to look at the sky, but he climbed down without hesitation. Eva distributed the rations—a lot of squabbles now, with everyone famished—and settled to a morning of waiting. Most of it she spent grooming Lana, who paid little attention, being obsessed by Wang, inspecting every hair root, turning him over and beginning again. Eva made occasional expeditions up the cliff, and now not only Sniff came with her. They moved around the wind-lashed slope above the ravine, nibbling the unappetizing leaves. The clouds were still low and dark and moving very fast, and the chimps were nervous enough to go back to shelter almost at once.

Around noon Eva climbed out again. Sniff followed her as usual, and three or four of the others. This time she led the way down toward the palms. There were fallen branches all over the place, many with succulent young tips out of reach till now. Eva fed for a while, then broke off a handful of twigs and made the "Come" sign to Sniff. He hesitated, grunted, and came with her, munching. At the ravine she climbed down and handed the food around, only a leaf or two each, enough to whet the chimps' appetites. They were hungry for

greenery and bored with being cooped in one place. Soon, in
twos and threes, they were climbing the cliff and going to look
for forage of their own.

Lana, preoccupied with Wang, was the slowest to move and
Dinks stayed with her, but at length Eva managed to coax
Dinks away, and Lana followed, rather than be left alone.
With Wang clinging to her neck she climbed reluctantly up
the greasy rock. Dinks had waited, and Sniff had been there
all along, watching the process under frowning brows.

As soon as Lana came out into the open Eva snatched Wang
from her back. He shrieked. Eva raced off, gripping Wang by
his upper arm. Behind her she heard the racket of a chimp
squabble, Lana's shrieks of outrage, joined by Dinks's, and
Sniff's hoot of warning. She paused and glanced round. Sniff
was closest to her. He'd put himself between Eva and the
other two and was following her up the slope, keeping them at
bay as he came. Dinks, in any case, was impeded by having
Tod to carry. By climbing fast enough to prevent them from
separating and one of them thus outflanking Sniff, Eva was
able to lead the others on right up out into the open, over the
ridge, and down to the corner of the enclosure. Not giving
herself a moment to hesitate she picked up the bag of chow,
put it between her teeth, and balanced herself out along the
swaying branch. She gripped the projecting end with her free
hand, swung herself down, and dropped. She'd been worried
that her weight coming down like that on the outer end
would loosen the fork from its mooring of boulders, but it
didn't, and when she rose and looked around she saw that
Lana must have already been on the branch, unintentionally
weighting it firm.

Lana reached the top of the fence and balanced there,
shrieking anger and fright and dismay. Eva made the "Come"
sign and held Wang out, offering him to Lana, like bait. For
the first time she noticed how little after that one shriek he

had resisted, how placid and uninterested he seemed. She placed him on a jut of rock and moved back. Lana still hesitated. Sniff by now was holding the far end of the branch firm, while Dinks was circling beyond, clutching Tod close, shrieking her outrage.

Wang whimpered, his voice hardly audible in the hiss of the wind. Lana overcame her doubts, swung on to the butt of the branch, dangled two-armed, and dropped. The moment she touched the rocks she scampered to Wang and began inspecting him for signs of damage, turning her head every few seconds to snarl at Eva. On the other side of the fence Sniff was herding Dinks on to the branch. Twice she refused to go, huddling instead into the corner of the enclosure, but he cuffed her out into the open, rounded her up when she broke for the ridge, and drove her back. The third time she did what he wanted—in fact, once she was on the branch she barely hesitated, but seeing Lana below busy with Wang just dropped and joined her.

Sniff crossed last. His weight on the projecting butt of the branch, with no one to hold the inner end steady, dislodged it from the pile of boulders, and as he let go, the spring of the fence tossed it back inside the enclosure.

While the two mothers calmed themselves by fussing over their babies, Sniff and Eva crouched side by side in the howling wind and studied the route ahead. The first part didn't look too difficult, a longish clamber across a slope of steeply tumbled boulders, but beyond that a rib of the mountain hid the next stretch and beyond that the angle became almost vertical, with the immensely steep slope of trees starting at the rim of a sheer cliff and rising into the cloud base above.

Sniff turned his head and grunted to the others to follow. When they paid no attention he went around and chivvied them from the other side until they began, reluctantly, to move. As soon as he let them alone they sat down and returned to their babies. In the end it was Eva who had to find a route, while Sniff herded the other two along from behind.

By nightfall they were barely half way there. In the dead ground beyond the mountain rib they had found a sheer-sided cleft, like a great sword-cut into the mountain, only about thirty meters wide but impossible to cross. There were ledges here and there that they could have worked their way along, but none of them seemed to match with ledges on the opposite side. They explored for a crossing almost till dusk, and spent a bad night in a sheltered gully. They ate chow and drank from a pool.

Eva awoke the next morning in a blaze of light. The storm had cleared the cloud rack away and the sun was shining almost straight into their sleeping place. The sea was rumpled still, but a dark clear blue under a paler, clearer sky. A lot of the grove had been smashed flat. The moorings of the airboat seemed to have held, but one of the flivvers was on its side and the old factory by the harbor had lost most of its roof. Humans will be busy, Eva thought. Wonder how long till they miss us.

She heard the howler two hours later, very faint because by now they were farther up the mountain, climbing toward the point where, now that the cloud base was gone, they could see that the cleft seemed to close. They reached the place at last and made their way down, still with immense difficulty. It was almost sunset before they were in among the trees.

YEAR THREE, MONTH ONE, DAY FIVE

Living wild . . .
Hunted, in hiding, wary from dusk to dawn . . .
But living free.

Wang died on the mountain. It had happened on the first day of freedom. When Eva had left to explore their refuge with Sniff, Wang had been alive, huge eyes listless, panting, and Lana had huddled possessively over him, not letting anyone near. There had been the choice then to give up, for Eva to make her way somehow down the mountain, find Dad and Gerda, the expedition vet, get them back up (but how? Wind still too strong for the airboat, flivver useless so close to this kind of slope) and by then Lana would be hiding, refusing help . . . It would never have worked, Eva kept telling herself afterward. It was probably too late anyway—once small chimps started to go, even in the Pool, you usually lost them. Months, even years after, Eva would find herself pausing in what she was doing, because the same old arguments had started running through her mind, with the same old guilt and sickness in her heart. By the time she and Sniff came back, Wang was dead.

Lana had carried the body all next day, grooming and cradling and inspecting it at first, but by the third evening she was just trailing it around by a leg, like a child with a doll. Eva managed to keep herself awake that night. In the pitch-dark, moving by feel, she stole the body away and buried it under some stones she had laid ready while she could still see. When

Lana woke she was puzzled, and searched around in a vague way but then let Eva groom her and be groomed in turn. Sometimes during the next few days she would seem to remember what she had lost and start searching and calling, but in a few minutes she'd give up and go back to whatever she'd been doing before. At no time did she seem to tell Eva, by look or touch, that she thought what had happened was in any way Eva's fault. Before the adventure was over she had completely forgotten. None of that helped.

What did help was having to stay alive, and free. Finding enough food took up most of the day. There seemed to be less fruit here than there'd been in the enclosure, perhaps because it was farther from the cocoa groves and so there was less chance of crop trees accidentally seeding up here and growing wild. Inside the wood you found that it wasn't one sheer slope but a series of natural terraces that had trapped enough soil for the trees to get and keep their foothold, so the floor of the wood was like huge steps, a narrow strip of soil slanting up to a section of naked cliff, and then more soil before the next cliff. To move from strip to strip you climbed a tree. A lot of trees and branches were down after the typhoon, and in places the tangle was too dense for even chimps to find a way through. There were two streams, which joined near the bottom of the wood and fell over the final cliff in a narrow smoking fall. Clinging to one of the last trees down there you could look out over the sea and the harbor and watch the flivver and the airboat rise and come and start looking for you.

On their first afternoon of exploration Eva and Sniff had seen a group of humans, tiny with distance, standing on the far side of the great cleft. From their attitudes they seemed more interested in the cleft itself than the wood. She guessed they were arguing whether the chimps could have crossed it. There were other patches of trees scattered across the rugged slopes of the mountains, any of which might hide the fugitives, and all of them desperately difficult to search in the damage after the typhoon. The humans would have to land a team from flivvers, somehow. It would be tricky, but they might manage it on the other side of this wood, where the steplike terraces ran out across the bare rock of the mountain face. Eva thought they wouldn't even try that until they found something to show that this was the wood the chimps were hiding in. The expedition hadn't brought any special hunting equipment with them, but they could send for it. What would they use? Heat sensors? Infrared-detectors? Something like that, but it would take them a day or two to realize they weren't going to find the chimps without, and then several more days to get the stuff flown out. By then, if Grog was right, other things should have started happening . . .

You could hear the buzz of the flivver long before it came past, and freeze. Eva made a point of giving the warning bark whenever she heard it, deliberately sharing her nervousness with the others. She didn't want them getting used to it. The airboat was more of a problem because if the wind was right it could turn its engines off and drift along the mountainside in silence. Feeding chimps created a good deal of commotion in the treetops, bending and breaking branches to get at the tender leaves at the tips and generally crashing around. The typhoon had battered the trees enough for the damage the chimps did not to show, but in the hour or so before the evening rain, when the wind blew steadily from the northeast, Eva kept a lookout in that direction while she fed.

The airboat came past as regularly as if it had been running on schedule, last call before tying up for the night. Eva would bark a warning, which Sniff would repeat, and the chimps would freeze, invisible among the leaves, and watch it float by. It passed overhead at other times too. On the second morning it hovered for a while above the cliff beyond the wood. Objects dropped from the cabin at regular intervals. Eva could see the people up there in silhouette, holding things to their faces—binoculars? A shape changed, became familiar—a long-lensed camera. When the airship had gone and she went to see what had fallen, she found the dark ledges flecked with colored spots. Bananas, oranges. They would photograph them and check next pass to see how many had gone. If all the fruit vanished into the wood, that would almost certainly mean chimps had gotten them. She did her best to warn Sniff with grunts and grimaces, and he got the message and refused to let any of the others out of the wood. They were all, in any case, by now infected with Eva's wariness of humans and other doings, and had enough to eat among the trees.

Next morning the airboat came back and checked. By then most of the fruit had gone, because a lot of burrowing marmots lived among the tree roots and scavenged around at night. (Later Sniff taught himself a trick of lying in wait on a branch above the burrows and dropping on them as they emerged in the dusk. Eva learned to gnaw the meat raw off the thin bones and didn't think about it with her human mind.) Several of the marmots lay around where the fruit had been, so some of the fruit must have been drugged. Eva guessed that Maria had the bit between her teeth again and wasn't listening to Dad. Okay, he'd been wrong about leaving the chimps in the enclosure during the storm, but not for the reason anyone had thought of. He'd have known the chimps would carry the fruit away before they ate it, if Eva didn't manage to stop them. What use would a drugged chimp be in among the trees? It would come around before anyone found it.

The fourth day, in the sticky stillness of noon when the wind was no more than a faint waft off the sea, the airboat came again. The whine of its motors stopped, and it hovered in stillness over the treetops. An enormous voice broke the silence.

"Darling, please, please, for my sake, please come home . . ."

Unfair! Unfair to both of them. Eva stuffed her fingers in her ears. Poor Mom, she'd be pretty well frantic by now. She'd know Eva was due to come into estrus in a few days' time— that had been one of the elements they'd had to consider in timing the whole expedition. Eva had already decided that when it happened she was going to let Sniff mate with her, if he wanted, which he presumably would. Why not? You couldn't choose some of this life and not all of it. The airboat passed on. A couple of kilometers away it stopped and hovered again. She heard the voice very faintly, not the words, only the tone of pleading. Poor Mom. There must be another patch of trees over there, out of sight. That showed they still didn't know where the chimps were hiding.

The sixth day, people came to the wood. They were lowered from a new flivver, larger and more complicated, which seemed to have no trouble hovering close in to the slope on the far side and letting them down on to a ledge. There were three of them, with ropes, helmets, rock axes. Two of them were clearly mountaineers, moving with confidence, balancing erect on the precipitous slope and helping the third one over the trickier spots. Just before they reached the trees this third man took off his helmet to mop his brow and Eva, watching from a branch three terraces farther down, recognized him. He was Joey, the head keeper at the Reserve. He wasn't carrying a rock ax but a stun gun. He checked the mechanism before he went in under the trees.

When they struggled in along the terrace Eva followed them while Sniff led the others down to the lower end of the wood. She didn't dare get too close, so only caught odd glimpses of what they were up to. They didn't seem to be doing real hunting, but spent most of their time studying the ground, presumably for chimp droppings and other traces, but they were out of luck. Because of the angle on which the trees grew, rising in tiers, somewhat more light reached the ground than it would have in a level patch of forest, and the going along the terraces was impeded by undergrowth, which also tended to hide the odd dropping that might have gotten scattered there. The hunters would have needed to chance on one of the places where the chimps nested or sheltered, and where the traces were much more obvious, but those were all farther down the mountain. After about a couple of hours they called up the flivver on a commo, made their way into the open, and were hauled back up.

That same afternoon Eva noticed two small ships moored out to sea. They carried their own flivvers, which rose and started to scurry unsystematically around the mountain. Both flivvers were caught unaware by the evening downpour and must have had a tricky time getting back down. It didn't look as though they were part of the main expedition. There was plenty of room in the harbor, but the ships stayed out at sea, riding the slow ocean swell. A new airboat came past next day, loitering under the heavy sky, with bright green bag and letters ABS painted in vermilion along it. ABS was a shaper company, one of SMI's main rivals. Uh-huh, thought Eva. Grog. Give us a month he'd said, if you can manage it. The way things were going she could have stayed out for years.

"You'll get world-wide interest," he'd said. "Okay, you'll have that already, but it'll all be under SMI's control. They can turn it off like a tap if they want to. But you make yourself *news* in the middle of it, and SMI can't copyright that. The rest will be onto the island like vultures, watching every damn thing they're doing. If they put a foot wrong, the world's going to know. They'll be everybody's baddies."

"They can sue us. They can make the Pool bankrupt."

"They'll never dare. I think you could bust that contract anyway—I've gotten advice—but it won't get that far. You've got a very fair deal to offer them when they come around. Which they will. Just give me a month."

"Uh."

Now Eva began to wish she'd done what Grog had wanted and smuggled a receiver into the enclosure somehow and brought it with her, so that she could pick up the news, find out how things looked from out there. All she knew was what she saw between the screening leaves. But the next day a different airboat came past, small and unglamorous but making a lot of noise because it was playing Tanya Olaf's song on its loudspeakers. On the flank of its bag was the broken butterfly and a message: THE WORLD'S ON YOUR SIDE, EVA.

There were a dozen ships moored out at sea by now and something passing overhead almost all day long. It became impossible to keep the chimps still while the watchers went by. It didn't have to be SMI who spotted them—any of the other companies would immediately send the pictures around the world, and then the rest would know. Eva realized that it had happened when she woke one morning and heard the noise, flivver-hum on twenty different notes and the deeper buzz of airboat engines. A big voice was calling from a speaker, and the Tanya Olaf music was blasting out full volume. She couldn't hear any words above the other noises.

Climbing cautiously up through the tree where she'd nested, keeping close to the trunk so as not to sway the leaf cover with her weight, Eva reached a point from which she could see several patches of sky. There was hardly a moment when one of them didn't have some kind of flying machine passing through it. Something came rattling and tearing along the treetops to her left, and a moment later she saw the bulk of an airboat blocking out one whole patch. Under its cabin trailed a rope ladder. It wasn't the SMI boat. Perhaps they were hoping Eva would grab the ladder and scramble up and give them an exclusive interview. Crazy.

Soon there were people being lowered on to the bare terraces beyond the wood. Climbers with light ladders and ropes
explored up and down for the least impeded routes into the
trees, and then the hunting groups made their way in, parties
of three, one carrying a gadget like a camera with a giant lens
as well as a stun gun slung across his back, and one with an
ordinary portable shaper with the SMI logo on its side. The
first man pointed his gadget up among the treetops and also at
any mound of fallen branches that looked as though it might
be hiding something. Eva guessed it must be some kind of
sensor that would register the radiation from an animal body,
hidden among leaves. They worked systematically along the
terrace while the flying machines buzzed around overhead,
invisible.

This was bad. She didn't know what to do. She had come to
the edge of the wood to watch the landing, and Sniff had
come too (he could smell that she was coming into estrus and
wouldn't leave her side). The others were farther down. There
were at least two parties of hunters between them now. The
chimps' whole instinct would be to climb for safety. They
couldn't work out they were actually better off on the ground,
provided they weren't on the same level as the hunters, because then the jut of the terraces would screen them from the
sensor. Eva had trouble enough to get Sniff to stay down and
wait for this group of hunters to move past, two terraces below. Then she and Sniff could move down behind them, and
join up.

She never got the chance. When the nearest party was almost immediately below her she heard the bipping call sign of
a commo. A man's voice muttered into the handset, then
spoke, calling to someone else a few meters off.

"They've located 'em. B Gang."

A passing flivver drowned any answers. By the time it had
gone the men were picking their way back along the terrace.

Eva and Sniff followed toward the edge of the wood and saw that one of the other gangs was out on the rock face already, waiting to be picked up by the flivver, ferried down the slope, and landed again. The SMI airboat was hovering close in with cables dangling, ready to moor. In the sky overhead thirty or forty flying machines maneuvered for a view of the hunt.

Sick in her heart, full of the sense of failure, Eva led the way down the terraces. Sniff came reluctantly, very nervous, constantly making small warning snorts and grunts. If he hadn't been so interested in her for other reasons, he would probably have stayed behind. She took a route she knew well by now, mainly from tree to tree without touching the ground. She had no idea what she would do, could do. Hide by herself? Grog had said he could still have used her if she'd been the only one to get free. It wouldn't be easy. She'd need to hunt for food, to spend several hours on that. She had to sleep. And anyway Sniff would be tagging along. Bright though he was, he wouldn't understand about the sensors. Besides, alone wasn't enough. For Grog it might be, but Eva knew that a lone chimp is almost a kind of ghost, not quite real. It was the group that counted. From the very first, she'd been determined to take Lana and the others with her. If they were caught, then it was all over.

Their route took them almost to the edge of the wood. The airboat was moored now, unloading what looked like nets. Yes, of course. You couldn't just stun a chimp ten meters up a tree—you'd have to catch it as it fell, or it could be killed when it hit the ground. So if the chimps kept moving, if she could reach them and lead them away through the tree-tops . . .

It wouldn't work. They'd be terrified already, with the bustle in the wood and the racket of machines above. Their instinct would be to climb as high as they could and cling. Without thinking what she was doing, Eva continued on down until she was only a couple of terraces above the one on which the men were going to and fro. Here at last she paused and tried to think. Her mind buzzed. She felt as if she were being wrenched apart, back into her two selves, but it was her human mind that kept telling her that the best she could do was go and join the others and try and get them clear and if she couldn't, then be caught with them, be shot, and fall and fail—nobody would really get hurt if the hunters did their job properly. Her chimp half simply knew it had to hide.

Something happened while she was still hesitating. Through the buzz of engines she heard a new noise, a cry from throats, a human cheer. Instantly she understood that someone had been caught. Too late. All she could do now was wait and watch. People came hurrying out along the terrace. There was a rope stretched out as a handrail to help them across the rock face to where the airboat was moored. Somebody passed out poles and canvas from the cabin—stretchers. The people hurried off with them into the wood.

Eva waited. After some while the people came back, slowly, struggling to maneuver the stretcher over the difficult ground among the trees. They came and went, in glimpses. She craned. Somehow there always seemed to be an obstruction, a bush, a tree trunk, the people themselves, between her and the pale canvas. Near the edge of the wood they paused. An argument began. Somebody spoke into a handset. Others peered out at the buzzing watchers in the sky above. A woman came scrambling across the rock from the airboat, carrying what looked like a sheet. Yes, of course. They didn't want the world to see them carrying a dead-looking chimp across the open surface between the wood and the airboat— bad image. The group parted to let the woman through, and now she could see the body on the stretcher. It was Lana.

Rage exploded. Eva didn't hear herself scream, wasn't aware of her rush through the branches till she saw the people turn and point, and a gun go up. The movement stopped her, changed the course of her attack. Even in the middle of the madness she knew she couldn't cope with people carrying stun guns. If the man fired, he missed. By then Eva was hurling herself out and down toward the edge of the wood, toward the open slope where the airboat was tethered. Perhaps some tiny part of her mind told her that if she could disable the airboat the people wouldn't be able to take Lana away, but all she felt was the need to attack, to break and smash and destroy. Anything human would do, and there was the airboat, huge and smug, trapped by its moorings on the rock below her. She picked up a loose rock and slung it. It bounced off the bag. Next time she aimed better and heard a crash from the cabin. The terrace on which she'd been hiding continued as a bare ledge across the rock face, like the others above and below, before narrowing and becoming just part of the slope. Immediately above the airboat it was blocked by a large boulder. Eva knuckled toward it, slinging loose stuff as she went. When she reached the boulder she gave it a heave, but it stayed firm. She started to scramble over it, looking for more missiles, but at this point she heard a grunt behind her, looked back, and saw that Sniff had followed and was bending to see if he could move it. She dropped on the far side, bent too, and heaved. The boulder stirred. They grunted and heaved together, rolling it from its bed and over the edge. It struck the rim of the ledge below and bounced, turning as it fell, straight into the cabin of the airboat, smashing clean through it and on in great leaps down the mountain.

Eva gave a great whoosh of satisfaction. As it ended, something slapped into her arm, just below the elbow, hurting like fury. She looked down and saw the dart of a stun gun protruding from her pelt. Before she could snatch it out she was in darkness.

Waking. Strange, drowsy, cold, the dream of trees . . .
Mutter and buzz and rumble—flivvers!
The dart!
Where . . . ?

Forcing her eyes open, fighting the remnants of the drug in her bloodstream, Eva saw nothing but dark mist with vague shapes in it. She thought for a moment there must be something wrong with her eyes, but then she heard a grunt, and a face came close to hers, peering into her eyes. Sniff. Every hair of the gray whiskers below his mouth had a droplet of mist at the end. She grunted a welcome and eased herself on to her elbow to look around.

Of course. They were up in the cloud layer. That was why it was so cold. They were on a ledge under a sort of fir with drooping branches from which dangled blobs of moss like seaweed, the shapes she'd seen in the mist. She knew the place. It was quite a long way up. The buzz of the flivvers and airboats came from below—fewer of them? Or just farther away?

How long? What time was it? The drug from a dart usually lasted a couple of hours. She tried to sense where the weight of the sun fell, the way she used to when she lay in the hospital . . . there. Early afternoon—that'd be about right. Plenty of daylight still for the people to find them. Straining her ears, filtering out the noise of the motors, she heard no sound of a hunt.

She felt decidedly sore. There was a cut on her thigh and bruises everywhere. Sniff must have carried or dragged her all this way, scrambling up from terrace to terrace, taking her with him any old way. Would he know about darts? Yes, probably. The keepers in the Reserve had to use them occasionally, and if Sniff had seen it happen he'd have taken an interest, tried to work it out. Good old Sniff.

They stayed together all afternoon. No one came near
them. When they looked for food they moved with caution.
The trees were different up in the cloud layer, with the fruit
unripe and little sweetness in the leaves. In the dusk, almost
by accident, Sniff caught his first marmot. Just before it got
dark they moved down to the warmer terraces below.

Eva awoke hungry but alert. No noises in the air at all—too
early for humans. Cautiously she climbed a tree and peered
around. The sky seemed empty, but there were a lot more
ships offshore, three with airboats tethered above them. The
sky was its usual sullen layer, and the sea dark and slow-
moving. Sniff joined her and looked around. They moved to a
better tree and began to feed.

They were still there when they heard the motor, an
airboat, not a flivver. They froze and waited. Over the wood
the motor cut out and was replaced by a burst of music—the
Tanya Olaf song. That stopped too. A voice boomed from a
loudspeaker.

"Eva, this is Grog. Your dad and I will be landing on the
rock face to the south of the trees. No one else will be there.
Can you come and talk?"

Starting and stopping its motor the airboat worked systematically up the hillside, repeating its message half a dozen
times. When it came into view Eva saw it was the one with
the broken butterfly and the message for her on its side. It
could still be a trick, she thought. You couldn't be sure of
recognizing Grog's voice, distorted like that, but she didn't
care. She wanted to know what had happened to Lana.

Sniff tried to stop her, barring her path and displaying at
her, and she had to calm him and groom him before he'd let
her go on. By the time they reached the edge of the trees the
airboat was already moored and Dad and Grog were waiting
on a ledge beside it. The sky overhead was even more crowded
than yesterday.

Eva hooted, but they didn't hear her above the noise of motors, so she lowered herself into the open and beckoned, then went back under the screening leaves and climbed on to a branch. Sniff watched from higher up, making little snorts of anxiety as Dad led the way to the foot of the tree. He looked absolutely exhausted. Eva reached down and took her keyboard from him when he handed it to her. Immediately she tapped out a message.

"Sorry. I had to."

"I'm aware that that is what you felt," said Dad.

"Sorry."

"Well, it's done now. I'm here in my legal capacity as your parent to tell you that I assent on my and your mother's behalf to the arrangement that Mr. Kennedy tells me you wish to make with your sponsoring companies, and which they in their turn have now agreed to."

"Is Lana all right?" said Eva.

Dad blinked.

"She's fine, as far as I know," he said. "Haven't you seen her?"

"Uh?"

"They never took her off the hillside," said Grog. "They got a change of orders. I better explain. Your dad's been having a bad time, and not just worrying about you. There've been some pretty severe personality clashes, with your dad being accused of everything under the sun. On one side he can't help feeling you've let him down pretty badly, and on the other he's threatened with the big legal stick for helping you set this up. Right, sir?"

"Forget it," said Dad. "Tell her about the agreement."

The bitterness in his voice wasn't quite real, Eva could tell. It was partly a kind of play-acting, putting himself in the center of the zone and extracting as much drama as he could from the moment. What he really minded, probably, was Eva's seeming to trust Grog more than she trusted him.

"It's really a sort of three-way, maybe four-way agreement if you count the chimps," said Grog. "World Fruit will set up a trust with the Chimp Pool as joint trustees. They lease St. Hilaire to the trust. They and SMI sponsor it. The Pool moves the major part of the Reserve out here. SMI to have exclusive filming rights, where possible by remote control cameras, and World Fruit exclusive commercial use of any such film. Human access to be kept to a minimum—we haven't gotten all the details worked out."

Eva grunted. It was pretty much what Grog had outlined to her in Mimi's apartment several months ago, not what she really wanted, she'd felt back then, when the whole thing had seemed so nearly impossible that you might as well daydream it perfect, with no cameras, no sponsors, nothing to do with the human world. Now that it was going to come true, she realized it was better than she could have hoped for. It was amazing.

"What happened?" she said. "Why? I thought we'd lost."

"Must have looked like that," said Grog. "All blew up bigger than I'd guessed. Your project director got a bit excited . . ."

"Maria went berserk," said Dad.

"There's been some kind of a power struggle in the World Fruit boardroom," said Grog. "Been going on a while—I'd heard rumors, of course—I've got a couple of contacts. None of them's interested in chimps as such, but what they do care like hell about is their image. This Maria woman is a protégée of a fellow who's part of a faction . . . hell, it's too complicated to explain, but what you've got to think of is the board members sitting around watching the pictures coming in from St. Hilaire, and on another couple of screens getting the figures for world reaction to what they were seeing. Not too bad at first. Nothing to look at but trees and rock and flivvers whizzing around. Lot of interest, though—they'd *loved* the stuff from down in the other wood. They'd gotten pretty much the whole world watching, waiting, wanting to see what was going to happen. And what did they see? Look, I've brought some stills . . .''

Grog took the pictures out of a case and passed them up. Eva leafed through . . . They'd been taken from above, at an angle, and all showed the same scene, the bare rock ledges, the bulge of the airboat's bag, its shadow heavy on the rock, the edge of the wood at the side. At the top of the first picture, black and tiny like spiders, two chimpanzees were knuckling out along a ledge. In the next the leading chimp was throwing something. Then they were both heaving at a boulder. Then they were looking down the slope, side by side. The boulder was gone and the bag hid what had happened to the cabin of the airboat, but the attitudes of the chimps spoke like a language—you could see their sense of achievement, their aggression and resistance, their sense of their own wildness and freedom. In the next picture one of the chimps was sprawled on the ledge and the other was bending over her, while in the bottom corner—the viewpoint had shifted slightly—one man was trying to raise the barrel of a stun gun while another was trying to force it down. The next picture showed Sniff carrying Eva back along the ledge. He had somehow gotten her across his shoulder and was knuckling along three-footed, gripping her left arm with his right hand. The last picture was a close-up of the same thing. It too spoke. Looked at with human eyes, thought about with a human mind, felt with human emotions, it almost cried aloud. All the old stories were there, the sort of thing people saw in cartoons and adventures on the shaper practically every day of their lives, the lone fighters against impossible odds, the rescue from the battlefield under fire, the comradeship in the face of death. Uh-

uh, thought Eva. People. They'll never understand. Not why he did it at all.

"Fellow who shot you had lost his head," said Dad. "If you'd fallen off that ledge you might have been killed."

"That's only part of it," said Grog. "One of my contacts told me that when those pictures came through, and the world reaction on the screens, the people at World Fruit as good as panicked. Some of them had been waiting for a chance like this, remember. They suspended the whole operation, replaced the project director on the spot, and went into a brainstorming session on how to repair the damage. My contact called me up and I got on to them and offered them this deal and they took it. So here we are."

Eva put the pictures between her lips and flung herself up to where Sniff was perched among the screening leaves. If she'd been able to open her mouth, she would have whooped as she went. He peered, frowning, at the pictures, turned them over, and studied their blank backs. She knew he could feel her excitement and happiness, but he couldn't understand the cause. She wasn't even sure that he could read the pictures enough to understand that the small black blobs were chimps, let alone realize that one of them was him. The human meanings, the stories of defiance and comradeship, would mean nothing to him at all. All he wanted was to move away with Eva through the tree paths, back into the depths of the wood, together. Eva gave him a chimp kiss, then detached herself and swung back down.

"That Sniff?" said Grog. "Won't he come and shake hands?"

"Uh-uh."

Dad was looking at her with an inquisitive gleam in his eye. He would have seen her rump as she'd climbed. Eva gazed blankly back. It had nothing to do with him, nothing to do with any human. Her feelings for Sniff and Sniff's for her were

not even like human ideas about sex and love. You mustn't
try and bring those ideas in. You must let it happen as it
would have happened in the forest of the dream, with the
human Eva no more than a guest at the wedding, accepting
and approving. But now Dad was probably wondering if he
could set up a research project. Eva reached for the keyboard.

"You can tell Mom I'm okay," she said.

Dad looked disappointed but shrugged. Bound to happen
one day, he thought. He'd want to set up a research project, of
course, as soon as a baby was born. He wasn't thinking of Eva
as his daughter anymore, any more than he would think of
that baby as his grandchild—which it wouldn't be.

"Can you face a press conference?" said Grog. "Sooner we
can get a commitment in public, the harder it'll be for the
bastards to cry off."

"Uh."

"Okay. I'll set it up for this evening. Down by the harbor
would be easiest—there'll be a fair amount of equipment to
fly in."

"No. Here. Under the trees."

PART THREE
DYING

YEAR TWENTY-FOUR, MONTH FORGOTTEN, DAY FORGOTTEN

Dying . . .
Sun high, warm on the pelt, but chill inside . . .
Yellow-gray mist, vague shapes, buzzing . . .
Time to go. Tomorrow? Next day?
Soon.

Crouched in the center of the clearing down by the old harbor, Eva waited. Hruffa groomed obsessively at her left arm, not understanding that there had been no feeling there since Eva's stroke last winter. Two years before, recovering from her first attack, Eva had gotten Dad's *Diseases of the Chimpanzee* out of the storage box and read about strokes. It had been difficult even then, with her right eye misty with cataract and her left too short-sighted to make more than a blur of the letters. She had managed it with the magnifying glass, but she couldn't have done that now. Anyway there was no point. She was dying.

The others knew. That was why Hruffa had stayed with her to meet the humans—she'd never done so before. Hruffa was shivering with nerves and was grooming for her own reassurance as much as Eva's comfort. Eva raised her good hand and began to search along Hruffa's shoulder, with her muzzle pressed close in an effort to see among the hair roots. She found a tick by touch, cracked it between her nails, and ate it.

The motor of an airboat drubbed from beyond the trees. Hruffa twitched with anxiety, and Eva pursed her lips and made the little sucking noises chimp mothers use to calm a frightened baby—noises she'd used when Hruffa herself had been a springy pink-and-black scrap clutching her side. The buzz became louder. She could sense all the others in among the shadows under the trees, watching. They too understood it was the last time.

Eva nodded to herself. She stopped grooming Hruffa and moved the hand to the keyboard where it hung in its loops on her chest. Extraordinary how her fingers still knew the letters that her mind seemed almost to have forgotten. Slowly she pressed a few keys.

"Hi, there. Just testing."

Hruffa jerked at the human voice. Eva reacted more slowly but more deeply. Over the past twenty years she must have gotten the keyboard out and used it dozens of times, hardly thinking about it at all, concerned only with what was to be said, not the voice that said it. Now, this last time, she was ambushed. The pang of ancient loss, a child with long black hair ice-skating in a yellow tracksuit. Me, whispered the ghost, the real Eva.

It was part of dying, coming in two like that. Hruffa must have felt the ambush, because she put her long arm around Eva and hugged her, rocking both bodies gently to and fro.

The airboat motor cut. It must be in sight by now, huge in the blue winter sky, but Eva couldn't see it. Higher-pitched, a flivver detached itself, hummed down, settled in a storm of gusted leaves on the other side of the clearing. Through her misted vision Eva saw the people take shape, two moving tree trunks tramping toward her over the dusty earth. By their movements and sizes a man and a woman.

"Hello, Eva," said the man.

"Denny?" she said. She had recognized the voice and was surprised. Denny was director of the whole Chimpanzee Pool, but he'd taken on being director of the trust as well when Grog Kennedy had started his mental illness and had to re-

sign. Denny was too busy, usually, to come himself, unless
there was something extra important. Then she realized the
humans probably thought her death was important. They'd
have known it was coming soon. The cameras were still there,
if any of them were working. The technicians hadn't come to
service them for years. After her first stroke the trust had
wanted to take her away for treatment, but she'd refused, just
as she'd always refused any help of any kind after the setting-
up stage. If the chimps couldn't do something for themselves,
it didn't belong on the island.

"Right first time," he said. "I'd like you to meet Gudrun
Alp, Eva."

Eva gave a grunt of welcome and held up her hand. She
could sense the tingle of excitement with which the woman
took it—she'd never touched a chimp before, so she hadn't
anything to do with the Pool.

"Hruffa," she said, and then because to human ears the
name would sound like a meaningless bark she spelled it out
on the keyboard.

"Hruffa, my daughter."

Hruffa held out her hand, unprompted, and the people took
it.

"Pleased to meet you," they said.

Few of the humans who'd visited over the years had really
come to terms with the idea of Eva's having children. Chimp
kids. In their minds there were images of white women being
carried away into the jungle by giant apes. They were both
uneasy and inquisitive. Once when someone had asked about
her newest baby, who the father was, Eva had laughed and
said she didn't know. There'd been a silence, a change of subject. Eva could have told them chimp societies don't work like
that, with a woman and a man falling in love and setting up
house. You could be fond of a particular male, excited even by
him, but your affection was for your group, and your love, if

you were a female, was for your own mother and daughter. Eva hadn't bothered to explain because that was not what the meetings were for. In her eyes their only purpose had been to get the project set up and, after that, to see that the humans stayed happy with things as they were and didn't come to the island except for the meetings. When people asked the sort of question people did ask, out of the endless human longing to know, she answered as briefly as possible.

"Your mother sent some grapes," said Denny.

"And her love," said the woman. Eva nudged Hruffa to take the grapes. Hruffa started a grab but remembered that this was a moment of ritual. She took the bunch and tore off a twiglet that she put into Eva's hand. Eva ate the grapes slowly, bursting them one by one against her palate. Last time, that shock of sweetness.

While she ate, the woman came and squatted on her other side. People sometimes did that, trying to conduct themselves chimp-fashion, but with them it had usually been a deliberate decision. This woman, Eva sensed, had done it naturally, without thinking.

"I'm afraid Lil's not too well," she said.

Eva grunted understanding. She held out her hand for another twiglet of grapes and when Hruffa gave it to her she passed it on to the woman, who took it and ate.

"Dying?" said Eva.

"She's got a few weeks left. She'll be glad to go. She's had a lot of pain."

Eva sat nodding in the sun, letting Hruffa put grapes directly into her mouth. The juice was as fresh and sweet as it had ever been in childhood.

"I don't know if you know," said the woman, "but a lot of kids have been taking their own lives. No reason anyone can give. I lost my own daughter five years back. Lil helped with our counseling group. I cracked up more than some, but Lil was pretty good to me and in the end we kind of elected each other mother and daughter. We had good times, considering. She never talked about you outside the counseling group, except these last couple of months when she's been getting old tapes out and playing them through and through. Then she asked if I could make it out here, see you. The trust laid it on. They said you've not been too well yourself. I haven't told Lil."

Eva grunted.

"D'you think I should?" said the woman.

"You decide. Say I understand. Thank you for coming, Gudrun. And for loving Mom."

Silence again. Eva rested. It had been an effort to press so many keys, to order her thoughts into a human mode.

"Trees are coming along nicely," said Denny.

It was just conversation, but he sounded as if he were trying to cheer himself up by talking about something that had gone right. And it was true. Eva was proud of the trees. She'd planted most of them herself, in the gaps of the old cocoa grove, using seed the trust had gathered and sent, food trees and shade trees. Most of them had failed or been smashed by a passing chimp in a temper, but enough had come through. Trees grew fast in this climate. More important still, there were saplings growing that Hruffa had planted, and Whahhu, and some of the others. Not all of them, but a few, because they had watched Eva doing it when they were small. It was something you did. Eva treasured the day when Hawa had taken her to show her a stem that had burst from the ground overnight, splaying its cotyledon leaves apart. Hawa must have planted that seed herself and remembered doing so and had made the connection. Yes, the trees were worth it, and so was everything else.

Denny coughed.

"I've got some other news," he said. "It's pretty important. Do you feel up to it?"

"Uh."

Eva felt very clear-headed, very aware. Though she couldn't see as far as the trees, her perceptions seemed to reach out all around her. She could feel the invisible watchers in the shadows, waiting.

"Fact is, they're closing down the Pool. Winding up the trust too."

"Uh?"

Eva wasn't surprised. The past half-dozen visits she'd sensed some kind of change in the air. And the technicians not coming to service the cameras—things like that.

"We've run out of funds," said Denny. "It isn't just us. There's hardly a project that hasn't got trouble. It's the same all over. You can't get a bridge built or a solar replaced. You can't get a road repaired. People won't pay their taxes. They won't invest or save. Some districts there's trouble getting the farms planted—just enough to feed the planters another year, that's all. A few kilometers north of where I live there was a community meeting last year where they passed a resolution to stop eating. Kept it too. Starved themselves to death. Nobody stopped them."

"My daughter joined the group that walked into the sea," said Gudrun. "They put rocks in their pockets, joined hands, and walked in, singing. Just a couple of dozen kids. Now they're doing it hundreds at a time. When Lil goes, I think I might try that."

Denny didn't protest. He took it as just one of the things people said and did these days.

"So it's no more of these trips, Eva," he said. "I don't know what it'll mean for the chimps."

Eva moved her hand carefully across the keyboard.

"Will they leave us alone?" said the young voice.

"No telling. No telling about anything. We haven't been here before. Sometimes I think it's just a phase, old Mother Nature, who we keep forgetting we're children of, just cutting the population back to a sane kind of size, and then we'll start again. Sometimes I think it's not a long step from walking into the sea with rocks in your pockets to deciding to blow the whole planet apart, clean sweep. I don't think that's going to happen. It'd take more organization than we'll be capable of much longer. I suppose there might be a war or two. Won't last. Nobody's got the will. No, funny thing is that the people who bother me most are the ones who'd try and tell you they're on your side. A lot of nutty little sects have sprung up, and we've had a bit of trouble in the trust from a group who call themselves Kennedyites, after old Grog. Their idea is that chimps are the human future. They call you the Inheritors. It's all mixed up with eleven-dimensional superintelligences in hyperspace, but there's always a chance some of them might trek out here and beg you to come back and save the world."

"Ask them to keep away."

"They don't pay any attention to me. Apparently I'm an emanation of Antitruth. I suppose you could try sending them a message by Gudrun . . ."

"I don't imagine anyone would listen to me," said Gudrun.

Eva bowed her head, collecting her ideas. She would like to send a message, she thought. It didn't really matter who to. One by one she chose the keys, concentrating, using the last little driblets of human energy. At last she pressed the "Speak" key.

"Hello," said the unchanged voice. "This is Eva. I am speaking for all the chimps in the Reserve. I want to say thank you to the humans for giving us back the life that is right for us. We are well and happy. We will be okay if we are left alone. I don't know what is going to happen in the rest of the world, but if the chimps survive it will be because of what you have done for us. Thank you."

She took the keyboard from its loops and pressed the key to eject the tape, but instead of taking it out she pushed the cover shut and handed the whole keyboard to Denny. She heard the click of the cover opening and made a rejecting movement with her good arm.

"Uh-uh," she said.

"She wants you to keep it," said Gudrun.

"I can't do that," said Denny. "It's . . ."

He stopped. It was as though he thought of the keyboard being still somehow the real Eva, but needing a chimp body to carry it around.

"Well," he said. "I suppose it might save us the hassle of trying to find a machine that'd play that size tape. You can't get anything these days."

Eva could hear the defeat in his voice, the defeat of humankind and all that cleverness, all those machines they'd used to control the universe, lost in the silence of a tape that had nothing to play it. She hunched her shoulders to the sun. She was going sooner than she'd thought. She hoped she wouldn't die before she got back under the trees.

The people rose.

"I'll give your message to Lil," said Gudrun. "And your love."

"Well, good-bye, Eva," said Denny. "It's been a privilege to have known you. Good-bye, Hruffa."

They shook hands and moved away, became tramping pillars, columns of mist, nothing. The flivver hummed and the downdraft buffeted across the dry earth. The noises dwindled into the sky.

Now Eva's own group came out of the trees, carrying the litter Whahhu and Graa had made. Eva's third daughter, Hawa, brought a half gourd of water. Eva drank a little and let

Hawa bathe her face while Hruffa handed around the rest of the grapes. There was a spat between Graa and Arrwa about the divvying-up but almost before Hruffa and Whahhu had barked at them they remembered where they were, and why. Eva let herself be lifted on to the litter and carried back toward the trees.

The others came out to meet them. She could feel their solemnity. They knew. Of course, they had not asked themselves if the humans would stop coming once Eva was no longer there to talk for them. There was no way Eva could explain something like that, not even to Hruffa. All she could do was let them understand that a change was coming—not by telling them but by feeling the approaching change inside herself, by sharing the feeling and her own acceptance of it. They joined the process, sharing and understanding. They knew.

There would be other changes that Eva herself had long foreseen but which there was no way of sharing. The structure of the groups would alter—they would become more separate without Eva's prestige to bind them. The dominance of the males would become more marked, and would shift slightly in other ways. Eva had always understood that she had to work within the grain of nature, her own and the others'. It had been no use, for instance, supporting Sniff indefinitely once Abel had grown into a big strong male and almost as intelligent. Poor Sniff had become morose and withdrawn, but it couldn't be helped. On the other hand she herself had always refused to mate with males she thought stupid or unsociable, and sometimes by guile and distraction had interfered in the same kind of way when the other females were in season. That wouldn't happen anymore.

The names, she thought, would probably go too, though not long ago Hawa had brought her new baby to her and told her his name, unprompted. Names were only slightly useful.

If you were in someone's presence you didn't need them; the other chimp was already an individual in your mind, a shape and smell and touch, a bunch of memories. Occasionally you might want to ask where someone was by saying the name as a question, and there were a few other uses like that—possibly just enough for names to persist, and the easy use of them to become enough of an advantage for chimps with vocal tracts slightly more adapted to naming to be the ones who had more children . . . hard to see how.

Fire-making, though. Knots. Making and using a bone needle so that leathery palm leaves could be sewed into a shelter and your baby stay dry from summer downpours . . . The litter on which Eva lay was of special importance to her. It wasn't the first—Eva had made that, years ago, to carry Beth from place to place when her legs became paralyzed. Later she'd shown the others how and supervised. Their main use was for carrying food and things like bedding materials up into the caves. This one had been made by Whahhu and Graa. Eva herself had taught Whahhu, and Whahhu had taught Graa. Graa, moreover, was a male. Eva had found him when he was still only half grown, high up in the mountains on a clear winter day, staring at the distant blue loom of Madagascar. Graa was Sniff's grandson. If you could make a litter, perhaps one day you would experiment with a raft.

No. It was far too soon. Generations beyond generations would have to pass before that, or before you could say that the skills had become enough of an advantage to be passed down in the genes, slightly nimbler fingers to make the knots, slightly subtler minds to think of uses for them, let alone for the new race of chimps to begin to move outward. Quite likely it would never happen at all—quite likely people would change their minds and come back and wipe out the chimps— but if it did those far-distant adventurers would not be Eva's descendants. They would be Hruffa's, and Graa's, and

Arrwa's, and Urff's—and Kelly's. Not one human gene would be there. Only, faintly, but in all of them, changed by them and changing them, the threads of human knowledge.

Our gift to the future, thought Eva. It crossed her mind to wonder what had happened to Dad. Denny hadn't said anything about Dad.

At the edge of the trees but still in the sunlight her bearers put the litter on the ground and stood back. Eva lay on her side in the useless warmth. If they'd propped her up she would have fallen. All she could see was a dark band between the glare of the sky and the glare of the bleached earth, but she could feel the presence of the others, hear their breathing and their mutters of doubt and concern. One by one, in no order, they came forward and crouched in front of her, panting lightly, putting their faces close enough for her to smell their breath and see the glint in the dark brown eyes. They reached out and touched her thigh or forearm or the back of her hand. The mothers helped their children to perform the impromptu ritual. The ones with small babies held them for a moment against her side.

When they had all taken their turns they drew back. Their voices changed to grunts of uncertainty. Eva was by no means the first to die—Beth had gone long ago, and since then there had been illnesses and accidents Eva could do nothing about. She had taught them to scoop a hollow, lay the body in it, and pile rocks over the place. But from now on, their voices said, everything was new. They would have to continue without her and survive.

In the end they left her alone to die. All of them, even Hruffa. She could not see them but felt them go, splitting into groups and families and then, like something happening in a dream, moving slowly away into the trees.

About the Author

Peter Dickinson was born in what is now Zambia. He was assistant editor of *Punch* for many years and is the author of many books for adults and children. *The Blue Hawk* won the Guardian Children's Fiction Award and *Tulku* the Whitbread Literary Award and the Carnegie Medal. His most recent books for Delacorte include *Healer,* the Changes trilogy (*The Devil's Children, Heartsease, The Weathermonger*), *Merlin Dreams*, and *A Box of Nothing.* He lives in London.